"What D[...]

Lacy lay still, imprisoned by her desire in his mind, to understand what he wanted.

David hesitated, not immediately having the exact words to reply. "I want more than a quick affair," he said at last, giving the only answer he knew for certain.

"We don't match," she protested, seeing nothing but hurt down the road for both of them.

"I know." His agreement was as realistic as her protest. "But I'm willing to risk it. Are you?"

The blatant challenge was something Lacy wouldn't have expected from David. The fact that he had made it showed how much he'd changed in the time they had known each other. The fact that she wasn't so quick to rise to meet it said the same for her.

"And if I hurt you?"

"Then I'll pick up the pieces."

Dear Reader:

Welcome! You hold in your hand a Silhouette Desire—your ticket to a whole new world of reading pleasure.

A Silhouette Desire is a sensuous, contemporary romance about passions, problems and the ultimate power of love. It is about today's woman—intelligent, successful, giving—but it is also the story of a romance between two people who are strong enough to follow their own individual paths, yet strong enough to compromise, as well.

These books are written by, for and about every woman that you are—wife, mother, sister, lover, daughter, career woman. A Silhouette Desire heroine must face the same challenges, achieve the same successes, in her story as you do in your own life.

The Silhouette reader is not afraid to enjoy herself. She knows when to take things seriously and when to indulge in a fantasy world. With six books a month, Silhouette Desire strives to meet her many moods, but each book is always a compelling love story.

Make a commitment to romance—go wild with Silhouette Desire!

Best,

Isabel Swift
Senior Editor & Editorial Coordinator

SARA CHANCE
Shadow Watch

Silhouette Desire

Published by Silhouette Books New York

America's Publisher of Contemporary Romance

SILHOUETTE BOOKS
300 East 42nd St., New York, N.Y. 10017

Copyright © 1988 by Sydney Ann Clary

ISBN: 0-373-05406-8

First Silhouette Books printing February 1988

America's Publisher of Contemporary Romance

Printed in the U.S.A.

Books by Sara Chance

Silhouette Desire

Her Golden Eyes #46
Home at Last #83
This Wildfire Magic #107
A Touch of Passion #183
Look Beyond Tomorrow #244
Where the Wandering Ends #357
Double Solitaire #388
Shadow Watch #406

SARA CHANCE

lives on Florida's Gold Coast. With the ocean two minutes from home, a boat in the water in the backyard and an indoor swimming pool three feet from her word processor, is it any wonder she loves swimming, fishing and boating? Asked why she writes romance, she replies, "I live it and believe in it. After all, I met and married my husband, David, in less than six weeks." That was two teenage daughters and twenty years ago. Two of Sara's Desires, *Her Golden Eyes* and *A Touch of Passion*, were nominated by *Romantic Times* in the Best Desires category for their publishing years.

One

Lacy Tipton crossed the bridge to the Island, leaving behind the well-to-do atmosphere of the Tequesta area and driving into the wealthy environment of old money. Jupiter Island was said to be one of the richest areas per square mile on Florida's Gold Coast. Although the true name for this lush winter playground was Jupiter Island, local inhabitants had long since shortened it to, simply, the Island. Whether it was an expedient form of address or a compliment to its residents was difficult to decide. Lacy liked to believe it was the locals' method of poking gentle fun at their prestigious neighbors for their well-known clannish tendencies.

The land in question was a true island, a slender finger of sand connected on both ends by bridges to the mainland and bordered on the west side by the intracoastal and east by the Atlantic Ocean.

One advantage of the power and wealth these people wielded was their almost fanatical desire to retain the natural state of their winter paradise. Only at the south end of the Island, before it became the community of Jupiter Island, did one see the condominium high rises that were so much a part of Florida's landscape. Yet, even then, the influence of the Island people made itself felt. Each building was a work of architectural art and a landscaper's dream. Although the lay of the land on the ocean side naturally hid the sea when viewed from the road, there was still plenty of room to see the open horizon.

Once past the buildings, a discreet sign announced the boundary of the colony known as Jupiter Island. Then there was an open stretch of road before the first winter cottage was reached. There was also a public park, Blowing Rocks.

Lacy Tipton eased her car into the small parking area and cut the engine. This was one of her favorite spots, a place she stopped at as often as possible just to enjoy the view and the peace of the outdoor setting. She seldom indulged herself with a break, especially now that the winter tourist season was upon them. The work load at her uncle's firm, the Tipton Detective Agency, had mushroomed almost overnight with all agents, of which she was one, carrying almost twice as many cases as a month before. Lacy sighed deeply, wishing the assignment she had just finished last night had allowed for four hours' sleep instead of two. She glanced at her watch. She had fifteen minutes before she was due at her appointment. Stepping out of the car, she walked up the sand dune. Australian pines blotted out most of the sun, creating a cool haven. The sea whispered softly first, then louder with each ebb and flow of the waves. The scent of the salt spray was captured by the trees, condensing it and adding the smell of pine and sea grape. Lacy inhaled it all, loving the state of her birth. The tide would be just right to enjoy Blowing Rocks at its most picturesque. She craned her neck, hoping for the glimpse of a sea geyser. Though her eyes sparkled with pleasure, she didn't smile. Lacy seldom smiled anymore. She had almost forgotten how. Not that she noticed, for she was generally too busy to see anything beyond the career that consumed so much of her time. Except for stolen moments like these, a holdover from her past when she loved the sun and the sea, her days were filled with her work.

She reached the overlook platform just as a particularly heavy wave crashed against the shore. The wind pressed her clothes against her body, outlining her slender form and the generous curve of her breasts. Ebony hair swirled about her face, for a moment hiding eyes the deep green of the pines that shaded the walk to the overlook. For a time she could forget to be on guard.

Lacy stood still, watching the plumes of spray surge up through the holes worn in the coral. Great geysers of water sprinkled diamonds in the air and painted miniature rainbows over the jagged rocks. Five minutes was hardly sufficient for more than a taste of the sea air, but it was enough to refresh her. Turning, she made her way back to the car. Her mind switched off the enjoyment, tucking it away. Anyone seeing her would have been disconcerted by the metamorphosis that occurred in the few minutes it took to leave the overlook and reach the car. A woman much like any other had enjoyed a few moments with nature. A person, eyes steady, movements controlled, expression guarded and fully alert to the world around her, got into a car and drove out of the parking area. The first had been someone a man would

have found both beautiful and interesting. The second
was still beautiful but infinitely more intriguing because
of the intense control. It would take a strong man, a man
who could appreciate depth as well as beauty and have
the patience to look beyond that which he could see to
touch the real woman.

A scant half mile later Lacy stopped again. Only this
time the choice was not a happy one. In fact, it was
downright inconvenient. A flat. She glared at the tire,
kicked it, then swore one short oath.

David Marsh saw her, his eyes noticing her figure and
liking what he found. Her car was broken down and she,
apparently, was not in a good mood about it. He pulled
over, deciding he could risk being late to help her. Getting out of his car, he walked toward her, seeing her more
clearly with each step. His first impressions were no good
at all, he discovered. What he had taken to be annoy-
ance over a minor inconvenience had been his imagination. This woman might have given that flat tire a good
swift kick, but not one hint of irritation showed on her
face. Her expression was smooth, too smooth to be real.
Her body was controlled, not rigid with temper. Curious, puzzled and more interested than the encounter
called for, he spoke.

"I don't think that's going to help much."

Since Lacy had been bending to rub the toes she had
hurt when she'd kicked the tire, she was hardly in a position to turn around. She tried anyway and ended up in
a very awkward and unbalanced stance. She would have
landed on her rump if his arms had not encircled her
body, pressing her close to a deliciously scented wall of
muscle. A rumble of masculine laughter wrapped around
her as securely as the arms that held her. Lacy lifted her
head and tried to push away, all in one movement.

The tactic should have gotten her free but it didn't. While the hands that held her were gentle, they were also definitely strong enough to hold her in place. Lacy studied the man more intently. She found herself gazing into the sexiest eyes she had ever seen outside a TV commercial. Light blue almost to the point of gray, they twinkled with amusement and male appreciation that made her forget why she had been trying to gain her freedom.

"Are you all right?" The voice stroked her ears like the finest velvet: full, deep and infinitely sensual.

Her stillness was uncanny, David decided. When she had realized she couldn't get away, she hadn't frozen or said a word; she had quite simply ceased to move. Her body was supple beneath his hands, neither rejecting his hold nor softening to it. His curiosity went up another notch.

"Yes, of course. You startled me. I didn't hear you stop." Lacy took a deep breath, surprised at the rush of words that had popped from her mouth. Anyone would think she had never seen a man before.

David nodded, released her slowly and stepped back. The wish to keep her in his arms was as puzzling as his interest in her.

Lacy inhaled carefully, strangely relieved to be released. The feel of his body against hers had touched a memory, a feeling she couldn't recall having had in a long time.

"Let's have a look in the trunk and see about changing this tire," her knight suggested.

Lacy trailed him to the back of the car, completely forgetting she was fully capable of doing the deed herself. By the time she remembered, he had his jacket off and the jack set under the bumper.

"Listen, I really appreciate this, but you don't have to do—"

Those eyes stopped the rest of her words. "Don't tell me you're one of those women's libbers," he teased, his gaze going from her dove-gray linen suit to the flat and back again. "I'd say not, considering your high heels and long fingernails." He stopped when his eyes discovered her hands. The short, pale pink ovals were a far cry from the elegance of the car and outfit.

"I don't have long nails."

"So I see." He shrugged, although there was a slight frown pinching tiny lines between his brows. "You should," he added as he turned his attention to the tire.

Lacy leaned against the side of the car, crossing her ankles. "Why?" She would not notice how smoothly he went about the task he had set himself, or the way his muscles rippled beneath the elegantly plain shirt he wore. He was a stranger, she reminded herself with more strength than she should have needed.

"I've got it. You play the piano." He looked up at her, almost hopefully. Another woman would have at least smiled at his banter. Not this one. He could see a flicker of interest, reluctant though it was, deep in her eyes, but still nothing showed on that beautiful, still face.

Lacy shook her head. "Not a note."

The frown deepened. "Guitar?"

"No."

"Type?"

"Only the Columbus method."

This time there was puzzlement in the glance he gave her.

"You know. Hunt and peck. Discover the right letter using one of three fingers."

"Oh!"

His smile was as sexy as the rest of him, Lacy decided, watching it grow across his face. Fans of laugh lines highlighted his eyes, and a tiny dimple tucked in one cheek while his lips parted to display even, white teeth.

"So what do you do?" he asked with a chuckle.

"I find things, usually," she replied absently. The man ought to be illegal.

"Funny, I never would have pictured you as someone who lost things."

Lacy blinked, finally focusing on the conversation. "Oh, I don't. At least not as long as I stay out of the kitchen."

"Can't cook?"

Lacy watched the tire slip on with ridiculous ease. The lug bolts followed in short order. "Not unless there's a fire extinguisher handy and a huge economy-sized bottle of antacid as well." She could tell by his expression he didn't believe her.

The hubcap was popped in place. "That bad? That's okay. I can't cook either, but I know a whole list of great places to eat." He lowered the jack without looking at her to see how she would take his comment. He had a feeling he knew. She would weigh him and then refuse. This woman did nothing by impulse.

Lacy was tempted. Oh, how she was tempted. If she had known a little more about the case, had a better idea of what her immediate future held with regard to work, she would have accepted the subtle invitation. She hadn't missed the Jupiter Island sticker on her rescuer's front bumper. As it was she had to turn his invitation down.

"You have someone?"

Lacy shook her head. "I'm involved in something that doesn't leave me any free time at present," she explained.

For one moment neither spoke. Regret showed on both their faces. Lacy had no idea how clearly her expression had conveyed her feelings. The man bent and picked up the jack to carry it to the trunk. Lacy followed.

"Don't forget to have that tire fixed," he said as he shrugged into his jacket. That one hint of emotion in her face had made him do something he never would have done. He glanced at and memorized her license number. He had a friend who would get him the information he wanted.

"I won't." Lacy crossed her arms over her chest.

He looked at her, then up and down the road. "I can't resist," he muttered as he pulled her into his arms and captured her lips.

Lacy gasped in surprise. He kissed her in a rush that caught her unaware. Before she could stop herself she responded, her tongue dueling with his as though they had been lovers for years. The kiss ended as quickly as it had begun. Both were breathless when they pulled apart.

"What did you do that for?" Lacy demanded as soon as she could get her breath.

"It was meant as a reward," he returned roughly. When she looked blank he explained. "Mine for changing the tire."

Irritation came almost as quickly as passion. Her eyes lit with it. "How dare you!" she said, using a cliché she wouldn't normally have touched with a barge pole.

"I would dare just about anything for a kiss like that. I don't suppose you'd like to try it again?" He took a step toward her.

Lacy's body tensed, her well-trained reflexes taking over. The man stopped, eyeing her. "You look like you mean business."

"I do." She relaxed, but only slightly. She still remembered how easily he had held her earlier. While she didn't really feel any worry, he was still a stranger. "I think it's time we said goodbye."

"Without exchanging names?" One dark brow kicked up in simulated surprise.

"There isn't really any reason to."

"What if I wanted to see you again?" He tucked his hands in his pants' pockets, studying her for a long moment. "I enjoyed our kiss. Didn't you?" If he watched those eyes closely, he could at least guess what she was thinking.

Too much, Lacy almost said, burning at the memory. His words did not endear him to her. "I must go. I have an appointment and I'm already late." She had the strangest feeling she had to leave, quickly, before she could change her mind and stay.

"Oddly enough, so am I." Touching his fingers to his forehead, he turned and walked to his car. A moment later Lacy watched him drive away, heading in the opposite direction than she was traveling. Shaking her head over the strange encounter, Lacy slipped into her car and guided it back onto the road. It took more of an effort than usual to focus on the business at hand, but she managed about the time she passed the small guardhouse that had originally been set up to block the south access to the Island. The structure was empty because the government officials had objected to the small community restricting travel on a public road. The action had been a controversial one at best, leaving both sides unsatisfied. The residents had responded with a tightly run police force that monitored every vehicle that entered its boundaries. None could stop on the edge of the street or enter a driveway without finding a police car investigating.

Lacy drove along slowly, watching the small signs set at the edge of each turn-in. She had a meeting with the Graysons, the first of the robbery victims. A glance at her watch told her she was twenty minutes late. Grimacing, she made a left and entered the narrow road, lined with red, yellow and pink hibiscus. Emerald grass surrounded the lemon-and-white trimmed house nestled in the trees ahead. The sparkle of the intracoastal that lay at its back added flashes of light in the shade of the drive. Lacy could not help admiring the view for a second before she got out of the car.

Daniel and Emily Grayson received her on the terrace, which offered a serene view of the intracoastal. Introductions were performed with charm and her apology accepted with a graceful shrug and a smile. Lacy found herself seated with a glass of mint tea at her elbow before she knew what had happened.

"I'd like to ask you a few questions about the burglary if I may," Lacy began gently. The couple facing her, with their silvered hair, without-a-care-in-the-world smiles and cultured voices, seemed so untouched by trouble or pain. She wanted to keep them that way. She had seen so much of the dark side of life in her profession that she valued sensitivity and gentleness perhaps more than most. She never used a hard word when a soft would do.

"Of course, dear. Anything we can do to help," Emily Grayson replied. "I miss seeing my Fabergé egg on the dressing table every morning. Daniel gave it to me on our tenth wedding anniversary."

Lacy nodded, as if having a trinket worth thousands of dollars on a counter amid pots of makeup were a com-

mon occurrence. "I'm sure it was lovely and very special
to you." She glanced at the husband. "Our client, Mr.
Garrick, contacted us this morning about the burglaries
that have been plaguing the area. As his security service
is responsible for many of the Island's residences, yours
included, he is most concerned." Actually, frantic would
have been a better description, but Lacy knew nothing
would be gained by betraying how worried the businessman had been. "He gave me a list of the missing items. I
understand that a set of small oils and your wife's jewelry were lost with the Fabergé."

Daniel inclined his head. "Some of those pieces will be
impossible to replace. Sentimental value, you know."

"Could you give me a rundown of your activities that
day?" Sympathetic, but knowing she would be no help
in finding the thief if she allowed her emotions to take
over, Lacy stuck to her questions. For one instant she felt
the increasingly familiar chafing at having to hold herself in emotionally. What once had been easy was now
becoming an effort. For five years she hadn't had any
trouble controlling her feelings. Until now.

Daniel spoke, drawing her attention. "A group of us
who had played golf and lunched together the day before had decided to take a trip to Fort Lauderdale and
take in a spot of nightlife and spend the night at a hotel.
The ladies had gotten it into their heads we were neglect-
ing them." He smiled slightly as he added the last bit.
"There were five couples in all. The only ones in on the
plan who didn't go were Jeff and Charles Osgood. Neither of them are married, you know."

"Are these all the people who knew about the trip before you left?" Lacy read off the names she'd copied
from the police report Garrick had given her uncle.

Daniel nodded. "All but the servants in the various houses."

"Did either of you notice anything out of the ordinary when you returned home from the trip?"

"The police asked us that." He turned to his wife.

"We didn't even realize anything was gone until my maid unpacked and I had my bath. It was then that I missed my dear little egg."

"You reported the theft then?"

"Not right away, dear." Emily Grayson spread her hands, looking old and a bit helpless.

"We had to check the house and see what else was gone," her husband explained, taking one of her hands in his. "That's when we discovered the rest was missing."

"And you didn't notice a door or a window left open that shouldn't have been? A track of sand on the carpet, something out of place?"

The couple exchanged looks. Both shook their heads. "We were too upset, I'm afraid," Daniel answered quietly.

Lacy could understand their confusion, and her expression showed it. "It's not pleasant to find out that your home has been intruded upon," she murmured soothingly.

"It makes one feel so vulnerable."

"Now, Emily, don't upset yourself. Remember, Mr. Garrick assured us personally that such a thing won't happen again."

Lacy's ears pricked up at that. She couldn't help wondering how their client could promise such a thing. That kind of rash statement could backfire and cost him more in the long run than the confidence value it had now for the victims.

"May I see your security key?" Lacy asked, when Emily had herself under control again. Daniel handed it to her without a word. "It works on all the doors?"

"Yes."

"Doesn't that become inconvenient occasionally?"

"A little, but until now it has seemed worth it."

Lacy stared at the small object, wondering if there was any way Daniel could have misplaced it or loaned it to a servant for a time. Surely in the course of a day or a week he would hand it to someone in his household to use. She said as much as gently as possible. The answer was surprisingly firm.

"I did not. The security team impressed on me how important it was that the key not be lent or left about. I even had a special key ring made for it. Quite a showpiece about the club if I do say so myself. We were one of the first to install a Garrick system, you know."

"What about when you and your wife go on a trip? How do the servants lock up?"

"I leave the key with Klaus, our butler. It is the only time the key is not in my personal possession."

A dead end there unless the agency could turn up something on the Graysons' butler beyond the clean slate the police and Garrick had found. Lacy sighed as she made the last note in her little book. Smiling, although she had little to smile about, she got to her feet. "Would it be all right if I spoke to the staff?"

Daniel rose. "Of course. Klaus will show you where."

Lacy glanced over her shoulder to find the butler standing in the doorway. She hadn't heard him arrive. Odd. The man moved like a cat.

The staff provided little more than the Graysons. No, there hadn't been anything or anyone unusual about that day. No, no one had noticed any doors or windows ajar.

No tracks, no bushes beaten down where a person might have entered or left. Nothing. Nothing except for one tiny thing. Two strange indentations in the sand halfway between the low and high waterlines on the intracoastal side.

Klaus had found them on the dawn walk he took every morning. Lacy strolled to the shore and found nothing beyond a pleasant view. She studied the beach. There was no cover for a boat to hide if the thief had come up this way. Of course, there were no houses across the way to see if there had been a boat.

Lacy headed for her next stop, still thinking over all that the Graysons had told her. And Klaus. She couldn't forget the man. The fact that he had not seen fit to mention the marks in the sand to the police bothered her. His explanation that he had forgotten about them in the confusion could be true but still . . .

Lacy entered the police station right on time for her appointment with Chief Riley. She had met the man once and liked him, so it was easy to discuss her findings to date.

"What do you think those marks could be?"

Riley leaned back in his chair, his trim body looking relaxed. The slow tap of his fingers against each other as he touched them, palm to palm, across his chest said otherwise. "Could be a pole of some kind, like the fishermen use to push the skiffs off the banks. There are quite a few sandbars in close to that part of the shoreline."

"I understand that your men patrol the beach in a boat."

"They do. Keeps the drug runners off that west shore."

"Wouldn't your boat have seen another craft?"

"Not the night Graysons' was hit. No moon. Remember?"

Lacy hadn't and berated herself silently for not having checked. "Okay. Supposing the thief did use a boat. That beach had a wide patch of sand before anyone would be walking on grass. Did your men check for footprints or the skid marks of a boat bow?"

"We did and got nothing but that butler's prints."

"What about him then? Anything odd in his background?"

"Only thing odd about that man is you never know when he's going to appear out of nowhere." Riley sat forward, propping his elbows on the desk. "I've checked every servant on this damn island, and there isn't anything shadier in one of them than liking a bit too much of his employer's sherry. Most of these people are third or fourth generation retainers."

"This is like hunting for teeth in a hen's mouth," Lacy muttered, making more notes.

"You can say that again." Riley's eyes narrowed in frustration. "I've racked my brains trying to figure out how that crook got his hands on those keys. It's the only way he could have gotten around that system. But none of the victims will admit misplacing it or lending the damn thing to anyone."

Lacy closed her book, tucked it in her shoulder bag and got to her feet. "There's an answer in here somewhere. There always is."

Riley stood up, giving her a straight look. "Well, I hope you have better luck than we've had so far in finding it. These people are on my neck about this. You'll make a friend of every man on this force if you get us off the hook."

Lacy held out her hand. He took it.

"You need anything, just let me know."

Lacy left feeling as though she had gained a bit of credibility somehow. She had half expected to meet with resistance at the station. After all, she was involving herself in a case that had started out as theirs. It was a pleasant change to find acceptance instead of the usual hostility. Now, if she could just find the answer they all sought.

Lacy left the Island lost in thought. The deeper she looked into this case the less likely it appeared. Someone, working for Garrick or for the victims or at the police station had a hand in the robberies. She could feel it in her bones. Her Uncle John had taught her the value and use of hunches. She played one now. Using her car phone, she dialed his private number.

"Have you sent a team over to Garrick's to interview the employees?" she asked, coming straight to the point.

"No. Why?"

"I want to do it myself."

"Again, why?"

"A hunch."

"Something you want to talk about?"

"When it's jelled better."

The verbal shorthand was their own. "Okay. Can you make it by two this afternoon? Or do you want me to have Barbara reschedule?"

"I'll make it. I'm on my way to lunch now."

Lacy had reached her favorite restaurant by the time she made her announcement. She swung into the parking lot and said goodbye to John at the same time. A split second later she slammed on the brakes when a white Mercedes coupe shot into the space she had been aiming for. Lacy swore softly and pulled in three slots down. What her exit from the car lacked in grace it made up for in speed. Irritated at the other driver's thievery, she stalked down the asphalt. A man got out. She stopped in her tracks.

"You!"

Light blue eyes gleamed with amusement as the man leaned against his car and folded his arms across his chest. "The last time I looked in the mirror," he agreed.

"You stole my place." The accusation slipped out before she could stop it.

"Did I?" He glanced down the aisle, seeing her car parked neatly a few yards away. "Doesn't look that way to me."

Lacy took a deep, controlled breath. She was overreacting, she told herself, regaining her composure. One did not shout at anyone in public unless one wished to look the fool. And while she had yet to raise her voice, she was easing in that direction.

"You know I wanted to ask you to have lunch with me today, but I wasn't sure my appointment would be over in time."

Lacy stared at him as though he had lost his mental facilities. "You're—"

He went on as though she hadn't spoken. "It never occurred to me that you would take a chance and join me."

"I did not take a chance," she muttered, glaring at him. The man was gorgeous, but also a certifiable nut case. Blast! Why did she have to notice his centerfold body now?

"Okay." He shrugged as he pushed away from the car. "My name is David Marsh. And you are?" He held out his hand as he introduced himself. Enjoying seeing her battle with her irritation and confusion, he waited. It hadn't taken him three minutes to realize this was a woman who preferred staying in control of herself. That she wasn't controlled at this moment pleased him in a way that he could neither understand nor stop.

Lacy put her hand in his before she thought. By the time her brain realized what she had done he had a solid grip that didn't hurt but certainly held her immobile. "Lacy Tipton," she replied, more in reflex than intent.

David grinned in a way that was guaranteed to put every woman in sight on alert to his interest. "A pretty name for a very beautiful woman. Remind me to compliment your father on his choice."

The masculine line followed by the unexpected reference to her family caught Lacy before she could fend off the pass. "How do you know my mother didn't pick the name?" she asked curiously. Her one besetting sin was her inability to allow questions to remain unspoken.

David urged her gently toward the door of the restaurant without releasing her hand. While he had the advantage, probably a short-lived one at best, he intended to secure her company for lunch. "Actually, I don't know. It was a guess. If I were married and had a little girl, I would have chosen a name to match her personality when she was born. I think women usually choose names for other reasons. Your sex is much more pragmatic than mine, I've found."

Lacy couldn't let that pass. She hardly noticed the hostess leading them to a corner table. "Do you think so? Why?"

"Send a man to the store for lettuce and bathroom tissue and he might come back with them, but he'll also bring a snack food or two, maybe a six-pack and a steak for the grill he insisted on having and never had time to use."

Lacy couldn't stop the laugh that bubbled to the surface at the picture he painted. When she had shared a house with John while he was her guardian, the scenario David described had been a common occurrence.

"Now a woman, on the other hand, might buy those things, too, *but* only if she needs them, has a coupon or they're on sale. Practical." Her laugh was music, low, deep and enthralling. He wanted to hear it again.

Lacy gave her order, surprised she had reacted to his nonsense. "We're sentimental, too," she argued.

He nodded, liking the way her eyes lit up when she was amused. "True, but again you're practical with it. You only keep the mementos of the men who are important to you while they are important."

"And men don't?" Lacy's brows winged upward as she awaited his reply.

David laughed. "Men will keep anything a woman gives them. Why do you think your sex gets so angry when one of you finds the souvenir his first love interest gave him fifteen years before his current lady ever came on the scene? Or the watch that says 'Love, So-and-So' when So-and-So was the woman of the moment seven months ago?"

"And do you keep your little mementos?" Lacy couldn't resist the question. Reminding herself she did not flirt could not stop her words.

David grinned, looking as pleased as the Cheshire cat. "Now that I'll let you discover for yourself."

Two

Lacy sat back in her seat, studying David silently for a moment. "You're taking a lot for granted," she said at last.

He tipped his head, not in the least put off by her comment. "Not really. I just believe in thinking positively. I am intrigued by you, and I see no reason to hide that fact."

"You don't even know me."

"That's easily remedied," he pointed out, taking a sip of his drink. She was fascinating. He had to watch her closely or miss something. "Go out with me tonight, and I'll tell you everything you want to know. We'll call it our second date."

"We haven't had the first one yet," she responded with a lift of a brow.

Grinning, he shook his head. "You wound me, lady with the pretty name. I treat you to a lunch in one of my favorite restaurants, and you say I haven't taken you out."

Lacy laughed. His absurd expression demanded no less. "You're a lunatic."

"I've been called worse."

"By a woman, no doubt."

"No, actually I think it was by my father," he admitted with an unrepentant grin.

The waitress arrived with their order, breaking the mood for a moment.

"So when can I see you?" David glanced at Lacy's ringless hands. "You aren't attached, as far as I can see, and I'm a reasonably attractive male, interested in you and prepared to indulge your feminine heart with a bit of romance."

Lacy picked up her fork and began eating. "I never accept dates on an empty stomach," she murmured, enjoying the banter enough to participate.

She couldn't take David seriously. His attitude was too lighthearted. The mood he created surprised her a bit. Her career had made her a student of human nature and usually a good judge of what a person was like. By looks and some indefinable aura, David gave the impression of being a rather intense, dedicated person, reserved even, perhaps a touch arrogant when the occasion demanded it. Nothing about him suggested this charmingly frivolous man before her. In a strange way what he was, compared to what she had expected him to be, disappointed her. She had never been impressed with fluff, even downright sexy, gorgeous fluff.

"You still haven't answered my question," David reminded her when lunch was over.

"What question?" Lacy paused, her coffee cup halfway to her lips. "You haven't asked me any in the past half hour. You've chatted about everything from sailing to the state of the union, but you haven't told me one thing about yourself or asked me anything, either."

"You noticed."

Lacy caught the gleam of satisfaction in his eyes. "You did it on purpose? Why?"

"To get your attention. To make you smile." He shrugged, his eyes no longer laughing.

Now Lacy saw the intensity she had expected to exist. The face that had looked so open and appealing was no longer. This face was smooth, quietly controlled, radiating strength and intelligence. This was the man she had believed existed, based on her first impression. She should have been reassured that her judgment had not been so far afield. Oddly, she was not. She had the feeling David Marsh would be far easier to handle as the charmingly frivolous companion she had shared a meal with.

"Now why would you want to do that?" she asked, playing for time. "After all, as I pointed out before, you don't even know me."

David looked at her in silence for a long moment. "That bothers you. My knowing that you needed a bit of relaxation really bothers you. Why?"

Lacy sighed in exasperation.

David continued before she could speak. "I saw a beautiful woman beside a road. She had a flat tire and looked like she could use some help. I stopped. She was still beautiful when I saw her up close, but she didn't show it. Odd, I said to myself. And being the curious person I am, I had to investigate. I couldn't pry, so I tried to make her smile. But I couldn't. She spoke to me, but she wouldn't smile for me. And I wanted her to, and think she wanted to as well. It was in her eyes."

He smiled slightly at her wary expression. "I met her again, quite by accident, and she had that expression on her lovely face again, and it bothered me. I kidnapped her in the parking lot and gave her lunch. This time I even got more than one smile." He lifted his drink in a small salute. "Was I so very wrong? Or is it that the lady doesn't want the rest of us to know she's human enough to feel? Or is it that someone somewhere has taught her to hide herself away?"

Lacy sat still, digesting all that he had said. She knew she wasn't as easy to read as he would have her believe. So the man was extra perceptive, better than good at interpreting body language. That shouldn't make her feel on the defensive. If anything, she should admire the skill he possessed. Yet she couldn't and didn't. He was right when he speculated about her dislike of being transparent. It had taken a long time to learn to hide herself, to become as familiar with emotional camouflage as she was with her own wardrobe. She had a personality to fit every situation. She alternately hated their need and relied on their effectiveness. But she wouldn't tell him that. No one knew how she really felt, not her Uncle John, not her friends and not the men she worked with. It was her secret.

"I think you have an overactive imagination," she murmured calmly, picking up her own drink. She watched him without seeming to. The disappointment in his expression was slight but visible.

"Perhaps," he returned just as quietly before downing the last swallow of his white wine. "That still doesn't tell me if you'll see me again. I have two tickets to the ball being given at the Island country club this Saturday. I was going to be out of town on business so I hadn't planned to attend. I'd like to take you if you're free."

Lacy was tempted, and not just for personal reasons. David was offering a perfect way for her to slip into Island society without causing a stir. "It depends," she replied finally, not prepared to decide on the spot.

"On your job?"

"A lot of things."

David reached in his pocket and extracted a business card. "This is my office number." He turned it over and scrawled another number on the back. "This is my home. I can usually be reached at one of these."

Lacy took the card, not certain she would use it. "And if I don't call?" she couldn't help asking.

"Then I'll call you."

"You don't know where I work, or where I live for that matter."

"I'll find out." David rose and dropped a small stack of bills on the table.

Lacy got to her feet, wondering just how her determined self-appointed jester would find her. It would almost be worth it to see him try. "Are you always this persistent?" His hand at her waist was warm and oddly familiar.

"When I need to be."

That answer had told her exactly nothing, Lacy realized later as she headed back to Garrick Security and her two o'clock appointment. When she should have been thinking about business her mind was determined to recall every detail of their lunch, every word spoken and all the questions neither of them had gotten around to asking. It was a strange feeling to interview each employee of Garrick's, record all their responses and still manage to remember how David's eyes had glowed in the subdued lighting of the restaurant, how deep and slow his voice had become when he'd said her name. Her concentration had always been so focused on the subject at hand. Suddenly she found she could and did operate on two levels at once. She even managed to detect a faint trace of something not as it should be with the last of the men she interviewed.

David's image vanished, not swiftly and certainly not easily, leaving her free to give her total attention to the slightly built accountant seated across from her. Samuel Mann. Company man for over thirty years. Married, no children. Lived with wife of thirty-five years. On the surface a person who liked security without flash, preferred a stable home and job. Reliable, conscientious. Nothing about him suggested or explained the faint tremor of the thin hands he folded across his chest or the way his eyes roamed the room as he entered. Maybe he was just one of those people who reacted to any hint of wrongdoing.

"I see that you've been with the company since it was founded," Lacy said, hoping to put him at ease.

Mann nodded, his eyes fixed on her face.

"Have you always been an accountant?" He hadn't relaxed one iota as far as she could see. Odd. Why?

Again he nodded and managed a word. "Yes."

"That's a long time to hold one job. You must enjoy it very much." The slight stiffening of his body did not go unnoticed. Lacy was getting more curious by the moment, but before she could probe further a knock at the door interrupted her.

Ross Garrick entered without waiting to be asked. "I thought you would be finished by now." He stopped beside Sam's chair, his hand on the older man's shoulder. "Hi, Sam. How's Sarah?"

Lacy restrained her irritation at the disruption. Mann had relaxed the moment his boss appeared. Whatever had made him uncomfortable with her was clearly gone now.

"She's just as always," Sam replied.

The resignation and pain in his response added another piece to the puzzle. Lacy listened, hoping for enlightenment. But neither man mentioned Sarah again as both looked at her.

"That will be all for today," Lacy said. "I might have a few more questions later." She tossed out the last more for effect than intent. The reaction she got was surprising. Sam froze for a split second, then nodded his head, a habit it seemed. Ross Garrick frowned and looked as if he meant to object but didn't dare. Neither man said a word. Sam left while Garrick took the seat he had vacated.

"Well?" he demanded. "Didn't find anything, did you? I told you and your uncle this morning that my people and the police have been over the staff with a fine-tooth comb. The thief hasn't got an informant here."

Lacy leaned back in her chair. The memory of the belligerent way Garrick had tried to control her uncle and keep him from assigning her to the case made her sigh. Sometimes the hostility she met wore her out. The very people she was hired to help often had difficulty believing she was capable of carrying out the simplest task. Men in her line of work still had the inside track because of the male image associated with being a detective.

"You can't be sure of that."

Garrick glared at her, clearly still struggling to accept that a beautiful woman could possibly haul his business coals out of the fire. "Damn it, I can. There isn't one of these guys who hasn't been with me since the beginning," he exploded. "I don't care if your uncle does own the agency and that he trained you and most of his people. He doesn't know everything and neither do you."

"Then why did you hire us if you feel that way?" Lacy kept her temper, out of habit as well as training. One of these days she would be judged on her ability and not on her appearance. While she appreciated her looks on a personal level, they were usually a hindrance professionally.

"I hired you because your agency is supposed to be the best in the business." He sighed, running his fingers through his hair. For a moment he didn't speak, obviously trying to regain control of himself. "Look, it isn't you. I know that a woman nowadays is supposed to be able to compete with a man. But my life is at stake here. I built this business up from scratch. These men, people like Sam, have been with me since the beginning. If I go under, some of them won't be able to get work because they're too old. I don't want that on my conscience."

Lacy always appreciated honesty. Because he hadn't pulled any punches with her, she would return the favor. "John didn't lie to you. I really am good at puzzles like this. What you see as a problem, my sex to be specific, in this case may be an asset. Measurements make great camouflage."

Garrick stared at her, surprised by the straight talk and the look that accompanied it. Grudging admiration flitted across his blunt features, and his lips twitched as though he wanted to laugh. Lacy nodded, not bothered by his reluctance to unbend. She had gotten what she wanted. Garrick was no longer a suspicious ally. He wasn't a friend, either, but that she could handle. She sat back in her chair, prepared to ask the questions that needed to be asked. This time she knew she'd get cooperation.

"What's wrong with Sam's wife? I don't see anything about a problem in his folder."

"It isn't in his folder," he said slowly. "The situation isn't common knowledge around here, and that's Sam's wish, not mine."

Lacy waited. He still hadn't answered her question.

Garrick read the determination to have an answer. "His wife has cancer. She never was strong to begin with."

"His hospitalization insurance is covering it, I take it? Cancer is usually a very expensive situation."

Garrick stiffened, on the defensive once more. "Just what are you getting at? Are you accusing Sam?"

"I'm accusing no one. I am doing my job. There is a thief. A damn good one. Too good. Someone has to be helping him. You want to find out who, remember?"

"It isn't Sam. I'd stake my reputation on it." He pushed to his feet.

Lacy rose to face him across the desk. "You are staking your reputation on it." Tucking her papers, notes and the personnel folders into her briefcase, she added, "I know it's hard, but you have to face the possibility that someone here is responsible for feeding information to the thieves if they aren't actually involved themselves."

"So how did it go?"

Lacy slumped in John's chair, eyeing her uncle as he poured them drinks from the small bar in the corner of his office. At nearly sixty he was still a trim, athletic figure of a man. His hair was silver, cut stylishly to match the expensive clothes he wore with more flair than many of their affluent clients. The women loved him, and his men would work for him until they dropped. In a world of artificial anything, John was as real as they came.

"It wasn't too bad. So far I have a butler who likes to take early-morning walks, a police force that's working diligently and coming up empty, a security firm that's more like a family than a business and a very nervous accountant."

John's hand paused at the announcement of the last. He glanced over his shoulder. "Reason?"

Lacy didn't have to ask which circumstance prompted the question. "I don't know. He could be one of those people who just get edgy when they face an authority figure. He could be worried about his wife. She's very ill. Cancer."

John finished making the drinks and brought them across the room. "Expensive business these days."

Lacy took a sip of the virgin piña colada that was John's specialty. "Very. The problem is I don't see how he would get his hands on the keys, assuming that's how it's being done. And even if he did, someone would notice. They guard those things like they were gold. And Garrick's isn't exactly Grand Central Station. Anything out of the norm wouldn't go undetected for long." Lacy sighed deeply.

John glanced at her, then reached in his desk for a white envelope. "You need some relaxation. A tired mind never solved a puzzle." He tossed the envelope across the desk. It landed squarely in Lacy's lap.

"What's this?"

"Open it and see."

She grimaced. "The last time you gave me something in an envelope it was a milk-run flight to New York. My stomach still hasn't recovered from all that up-and-down flying."

"You'll like this better. I promise."

Lacy opened the envelope. The heavily embossed ticket slipped out faceup. Reading it was no problem; believing it was. "I never have put much faith in coincidences."

John lifted his head alertly, something in her tone piquing his interest. His eyes narrowed, watching her intently. Accidents and coincidences always made him wary. "Just what sort of coincidence are we talking about?"

Lacy tapped the invitation against her fingers. "You're the second man who wants to see me at this party."

"Who was the first?"

"David Marsh. If the sticker on his car and the fact he has two tickets to this do is any indication, he's a resident."

"I hope you said yes." At her slow shake of the head, he frowned. "Why not? This kind of an entrée could be invaluable. Neither of us believes this thief works without help. His accomplice could be someone on the Island. A social setting could provide you with an opportunity to catch someone off guard. It isn't like you to miss this kind of a chance." He eyed her sharply. "Unless there's something about the man you aren't telling me."

Lacy wasn't about to admit to anyone how David affected her. She didn't even want to admit it to herself. She eyed the ticket as though it would bite. "I like dancing as much as the next woman, but other than David I don't know anyone at this bash. And you know yourself how clannish these people are." It was a lame excuse at best.

Thinking she was teasing, John laughed and tossed a credit card in her lap. "I knew I trained you right. Quit trying to give an old man an attack. Buy something elegant and sexy. You know how you like clothes. It will

make you feel better and make it easier for you to blend
in. Charge it to the firm. Uniform of the day."

Lacy picked up the card, for one moment hiding her
expression from John. He was right. She had to go, and
having David along would give her the entrée she needed.
She had to attend even if she didn't like it. "This is going
to cost you a mint," she promised, half meaning it. She
needed something to take her mind off what she was
about to do. How she hated lies, even little ones.

"I know I will. I haven't forgotten how much you enjoy indulging your taste for fashion and style. I can't wait
to see what you buy."

"I'll call David Marsh and tell him I changed my
mind." Lacy finished her drink as though it didn't matter to her one way or another.

"It would be better than going alone." He frowned as
though he had caught a hint of something he didn't understand. "This man is all right, isn't he?" He lifted a
brow curiously.

Lacy recognized the look. John had never pried into
her life even when she had lived as his ward for the three
years before she'd come of age. He believed in letting her
make her own decisions. Leaning forward, she slid the
ticket across the desk. "I won't need this."

"You're sure? I'm not pushing you?"

"When have you ever?" Lacy rose slowly, stretching
slightly. It had been a long day, and it still wasn't over.

John walked out with her. They were the last ones to
leave, a common occurrence since the day Lacy had
joined the business. "Tell me about this Marsh," John
invited carefully. "Sometimes I wonder if I did the right
thing in letting you join the agency. Maybe I should have
encouraged you in a more conventional direction."

Lacy got into the car, glaring up at her uncle in mock irritation. "I know what you're getting at, you old scoundrel. Don't pretend to want to bounce baby-powdered bottoms on your knee. You never were the type, if you recall. When all my friends had families encouraging them to find nice secure niches, you were teaching me the ropes here. I've never objected to working here, have I?"

Lately, John seemed to have developed a split personality. On the job he cared for her performance and nothing else. But recently he had begun taking an interest in her private life. He now made no secret that he wouldn't mind seeing her in a permanent relationship. Nothing Lacy had said on the subject thus far had convinced him that she was comfortable with her world just the way it was.

"But I never have asked you outright. Do you regret it?" He had to know.

"You know I don't. There is nothing I would rather be doing with my life." If the second sentence lacked the conviction of the first, only she heard it. "I love the challenge and the variety." Well, at least most of the time she did. "I can't imagine giving it up for anything or anyone." She grinned impudently as she shut the door. "So forget the home, successful career and diaper lecture and worry about your credit rating when I get finished with my shopping trip."

Lacy didn't wait to hear John's groan before driving away. She couldn't help thinking of David as she headed for home. It appeared she would be using the card he had given her after all. With the ball only a few days away, she should call him tonight. She debated telling him why she had agreed and decided against that course. Her job was by no means secret, but she wasn't certain she wanted to handle the inevitable questions her occupation always generated.

For once it would be nice to get to know someone before telling them she was a private detective. If all she got was one night of being just plain Lacy Tipton, she would be satisfied. With that settled, Lacy relaxed slightly, again aware of the exhaustion that had been dogging her footsteps of late. Usually she could handle the rush of the tourist season with ease. But for some reason this year she was finding it tough going.

Tipton's was like any other Florida business, booming from Thanksgiving to Easter, which was why she needed the quiet life she led outside the office. Sometimes she desperately wanted a place to unwind. That was what had attracted her to the town house complex near the ocean. The security of the closed community protected her from solicitors and petty crime while the setting was a small slice of paradise with a beautiful beach only a three-minute walk from her front door. There was a club-house and pool she rarely used, preferring the sea or the serenity of the garden she had planned and planted in the postage stamp-sized backyard.

As usual, Lacy kicked off her shoes as soon as she stepped in the front door. Impractical off-white carpet covered every inch of floor. Sunset-peach walls rose to high beamed ceilings. There was no clutter to detract from the basic lines of each room, nor was the furniture meant to call attention to itself. Instead, each piece was built for comfort. The indirect lighting, provided by strategically placed ceiling- and floor-mounted fixtures, was an extension of the retreat effect and very unusual. Everything about Lacy's home spoke of sensitivity to atmosphere.

What it didn't speak of was her complete inability to cook or clean. For all her savvy on the job, for all her training in various arts that required intense and complete coordination, Lacy was incapable of putting the simplest meal together without burning ninety percent of it. A vacuum was a device created by Satan to chew up electrical cords or blow fuses. She could unstop a sink, but she couldn't wash clothes in a machine without turning something a putrid shade of pink or orange. In short, Lacy was a domestic disaster. So, she had a maid in once a week, patronized the best of the take-away food places and knew by heart the menu of the frozen meal section of the local grocery. Tonight's selection was turkey pot-pie, broccoli au gratin and a piece of chocolate cake thawed in the microwave.

She took a long bath. Then she treated herself to a glass of wine on the patio. She still hadn't used up more than two hours. Lacy eyed the phone beside her chair, knowing she couldn't put off calling David any longer. He answered on the second ring, almost as though he had been sitting next to the phone, waiting.

"Is that invitation still open?" she asked without identifying herself.

"Did you think I'd extend it to a dozen women just to make sure I had a date?" he replied.

"No, I suppose not." Lacy paused, then said, "Would seven be too early for you to pick me up?"

His voice was as smooth and deep on the phone as it was in person. "Six would be even better."

"Why? The ball doesn't start until eight."

"True, but I thought we could stop by here before we bearded the social lions in their den."

Lacy thought the idea over slowly. She wasn't sure how she felt about seeing his house. She had to admit to being curious about him. Being in his home was bound to provide more clues to his personality. Yet it also smacked of a faster paced relationship than she was prepared to deal with at this moment in her life.

"Scared, Lacy?" David murmured when she didn't answer. He was banking on her reacting to the challenge rather than being put off by it.

"Of what?" she returned, sitting up straight in her chair.

"You tell me. Surely it doesn't take that long to answer a simple question."

"No, but it does take that long to go over my schedule to see if I can get home and change in so little time. I usually work long hours." Before he could ask at what, she hurried on. "I think I can make it. Just."

David sighed soundlessly in relief. For a moment there she'd had him worried. He wanted to spend more time with this woman, to learn about her, to slip behind the veil of secrecy that seemed to cling to her skin like mist from the sea.

"Good. I'll see you then."

"Don't you want my address?" Lacy demanded, realizing he intended to hang up.

"I have it." He waited for her reaction. Would she be angry?

"How?"

"Department of Motor Vehicles."

"They don't provide that kind of service." Actually they did, but only in very special cases, or if a person knew the right people.

"I can be very persuasive."

"Also underhanded." Lacy couldn't help being pleased and intrigued at his interest and his single-mindedness.

"Aren't you flattered I tracked you down? Most women would be."

"I'm not most women." Her reply was automatic and without heat. She was more intent on getting a handle on one David Marsh. "Just who are you?"

David laughed, a deep, husky throb of amusement that could beguile the unwary. Lacy felt like poking her fingers in her ears for protection.

"That's a strange question to ask a man with whom you have just agreed to spend the evening. Who do you think I am?"

"I don't know, but I intend to find out," she mumbled without thinking.

"Now that sounds promising. I can't wait until you begin investigating me," he whispered, teasing her a little.

Lacy stiffened at the innocent comment. Or was it innocent? Could he know who and what she was? He had certainly found her address quickly enough. She couldn't ask, so she did the only thing she could do. She played along.

"Surely that depends on what you have to hide."

"Since I am basically honest, upstanding and a contributing member of society, I don't think I have anything to fear. So I'll chance it." With that he hung up the phone. It was always a good strategy to leave a person guessing, especially a woman like Lacy who seemed to have more than her fair share of curiosity.

Three

"My Lord, Lacy! I know I said you could buy a dress, but are you sure you didn't buy a dress store." John frowned darkly at the receipt Lacy had just handed him.

Lacy grinned, not taken in by his grumbling. "One dress is all I bought. You don't want me going to this posh party looking like Cinderella before the fairy godmother, do you?" She stretched her legs out in front of her and crossed her hands over her stomach. "Besides, I needed a lift. This case isn't moving at all. In the past few days I've talked to both sets of victims, gone over the grounds, been back to Garrick's twice and eliminated a possible suspect, the Grayson butler, and still nothing adds up."

"Is that any reason to stick me with this kind of bill?" John growled, stuffing the hated paper into his drawer, which he then slammed with a bang. He wasn't really angry or even mildly irritated. Lacy had used the purchase of the gown for the Island ball as a way to let off steam. This grumbling was his method for doing the same. Both played the game, knowing exactly what the other was doing.

"So, hotshot, tell me what you do have." John copied Lacy's relaxed position.

Lacy sighed deeply. "Precious little."

"Hunches?"

"A few."

"Care to share them?"

Staring off into space, Lacy considered that. John had a right to know. Perhaps he could even add something to the tiny leads she had uncovered. Yet the feelings that she was going on at present were so nebulous that she wasn't certain they would stand the strain of words.

"That bad, huh?"

Lacy focused on his face. "I can see why Riley hasn't come up with anything. So far all I've been able to figure out for certain is that the thief is arriving and leaving by boat. But what kind, whose or where it's docked is anyone's guess. How does he slip by the police craft that patrols that stretch? I tried it last night and got caught twice."

"Maybe they're more careful now because of the robberies." John offered the solace without really believing it. Riley was a good cop. His force was well paid. His men were good, damn good. Jupiter Island wasn't large, and the accesses to it were limited to a single road on land, the intracoastal on the west side and the ocean on the east. The houses were clustered in the small area, making an undetected entry even more difficult, which was why there had been so few thefts and problems to date.

"I'm sure they were, but I'm no slouch where boats are concerned, and last night was so cloudy that there was no moon and no one on the water but us. They still caught me." She shifted, remembering the polite but firm way the officers had insisted on taking her to the station. They had listened to her but had also called Chief Riley to check out her story. "Those guys were extremely efficient. Whoever our crook is, he's good."

John ignored her comment about the thief's prowess, sticking to his own train of thought. "If our man is taking a boat in, why aren't there any footprints in the sand? I thought you told me that beach was too wide for him to jump from the craft to the grass."

"It is. I have a feeling those marks the Graysons' butler found were for some kind of pole. You know the kind that fishermen use to push flat-bottomed boats along the mud flats. A person could use that like a pole-vaulter if he or she were athletically inclined."

Admiration for her deduction flickered briefly in John's eyes. "So we're looking for someone who is very fit...." John paused, suddenly struck by an idea. Before he could speak, Lacy did.

"There is only one flaw with that possibility. How the devil does the thief get from the bank to the boat? The boat to the bank is easy. I tried that this morning. But it's almost impossible to go the other way. The only way it works is to jump into the water beside the boat then climb in."

"Which is why he only takes small, easily portable items," John concluded. "He wouldn't want to take a chance on dropping something or getting overbalanced himself. A man-size object falling in the water at night makes a fairly loud noise. No one would mistake such a sound for a fish jumping."

Lacy inclined her head before going on with her deductions. "And then there's the little matter of the keys.

One key per householder unless it's a couple. One master set in a vault at Garrick's with only Ross having access. So unless we suspect him, there's no way our thief could get hold of a key without going through the owners. And they're positive their keys haven't been missing, misplaced or loaned. Dead end.''

Lacy pushed upright in her chair and continued. ''The consensus of opinion at Garrick's and the police department is that it's one of the servants or some regular outside help. But that's all supposition, and none of it gets us much at this point.''

''I take it you don't agree.''

''No, I don't. So far I haven't found one regular employee on that island who has extra unexplained funds or even a motive. On top of that, every one of those people seem to have been there since the year one. The shortest record of employment is five years.''

''Maybe you'll find something at the ball. Did you call Marsh?''

''I was wondering how long it was going to take you to ask me that,'' Lacy murmured, her body tensing slightly. ''Yes, I called David, and he's taking me.''

''So that's why the gold-plated dress,'' John teased.

Lacy shrugged. She wasn't about to admit to anyone that she had twisted and turned in front of a dozen mirrors, wondering if the beautiful gowns she tried on would appeal to one David Marsh. It had taken three stores before she would even admit it to herself. ''Could be, but I'll never tell.''

''I think I want to meet this man. What does he do for a living?'' John hadn't gotten where he was without being able to see more than most people would be comfortable with, and he knew his niece.

Lacy rolled her eyes. Fooling John was nearly impossible. "You aren't going anywhere near him if you're going to play the heavy-handed guardian," she replied, giving him a look that spoke volumes.

John chuckled, spreading his hand in a gesture that could have meant innocence or intent. "Now, Lacy..."

Lacy stood up, propping her hands on her hips. "Don't you 'now, Lacy' me, Uncle Jonathan Michael Leeland Tipton. The last time you said that was before that poor boy wanted to take me out all night for my senior prom. I missed a fancy Fort Lauderdale nightclub show because of you."

John managed a shamefaced expression, although it sat ill on his aristocratic features. "That kid had no nerve."

"That kid was eighteen years old and up against a gentle tyrant who looked like an elegant tough."

He couldn't control the pride that swelled his chest at her description. Lacy saw it and grinned. "Got you with that, did I? I always knew you had an ego the size of Florida."

"Do not," he returned, reaching for his briefcase. Throwing his jacket over his arm, he walked with Lacy out of the office. "You're just trying to divert me."

"And succeeding, too," she shot back as they reached the parking lot.

John stopped her with a hand on her arm. "I really would like to meet this guy," he said quietly, abruptly sober.

"We'll see," Lacy responded, touching his hand. She wasn't sure what part, if any, David would play in her life, and until she was she saw no reason to bring the two men together. "You are my best and favorite relative." Impulsively, she leaned forward and kissed his cheek.

"Dad would have been proud of what a good father you made for me when he wasn't here to do the job himself."

John blinked quickly before he disgraced himself. "I didn't do so bad for a confirmed bachelor, did I?"

"We make a good team. You've always told me so. But right now this member of the Tipton duo is going home. I've still got a couple of hours work ahead of me before I can hit the sack."

"No date?" John frowned, not liking that bit of news. "I wish you would get out more. You're never going to get a man if you don't exert yourself a little," he mumbled.

She shook her head. His continued determination to get someone in her life was a direct contrast to his passionate belief in his own freedom. "I tell you what. You find yourself a nice lady willing to take you on, and I'll find myself someone...." She paused a second.

"Like David Marsh maybe?" he finished for her, teasing her and at the same time doing a little subtle prying.

"Maybe. He's certainly sexy enough to turn any woman's head." Lacy had spoken without thinking.

John's expression lightened miraculously. This was the first time he had ever heard Lacy admit to finding a man attractive. Usually she was as close as a clam. "You mean it?" Then he frowned again when the conditions of her mate-seeking penetrated his mind. "I don't want a woman," he grumbled. At her skeptical look he explained more carefully. "At least not in that capacity."

Lacy laughed. "I don't know why not. After all, you aren't getting any younger." His scowl was a picture of masculine affront that increased Lacy's amusement.

"I'm beginning to think I pity David Marsh if you did take a real liking to the man. You'd lead him a chase just for the sport of it," he muttered. He opened her car door. "Maybe I didn't do such a hot job as a surrogate father after all. When a female doesn't know her own duty to home and hearth, then the world is in sad shape."

Lacy patted his hand. If she had thought he'd meant his outrageous comment, she would have been angry. But she knew better. John was a great believer in person power, having no built-in prejudice at all. "I'm such a disappointment to you," she agreed with a sympathy they both knew was false.

His only reply was a grunt and a slam of the door he still held open. She watched him saunter off, his upright carriage and agile stride belying his fifty-nine and a half years. Love softened her features for the man who had taken in a very precocious sixteen-year-old and raised her without any help from a wife. To this day she had no idea how he had managed to know what she needed and to be there when it was important while leaving her to find her own way when that, too, was necessary. Even now he offered his support without forcing it on her.

The phone was ringing when Lacy arrived home. It was David.

"What are you doing tonight?" he asked almost before Lacy had finished saying hello.

"Relaxing, doing a bit of work before an early night. Why?" Lacy replied as she kicked off her shoes and sat down. The pleasure of hearing his voice made her want to curl up in the chair and chat for hours.

"How about dinner? Have you had it yet?"

"No, but—"

"Good. How do you feel about steaks and a bottle of wine?" He waited impatiently, hoping she would agree. The silence said she wouldn't. "I could come to you if you would rather." It wasn't the way he had planned it, but if a change in location would get him her company, he would gladly cart his cook and the food to her house.

Lacy didn't want company tonight, even David's. She had just spent a long and fruitless week, searching for needles in the sand. She needed some time alone to unwind. And, more importantly, she had work to do.

"Could I take a rain check?" she asked, real regret in her voice.

David frowned, more than disappointed at her refusal. He wanted to coax her to change her mind, and that surprised him. He had always taken a woman at her word. It had never been his way to push. Yet he wanted to push now. Only the memory of the wariness that Lacy seemed to wear like a cloak kept him silent. He glanced across the room to the expensive bottle of wine he had brought from the wine cellar. It had taken him ten minutes to decide which vintage to offer her. He had wanted to give her a night of relaxation and fun, things he was almost certain she had little of. He wanted to see her smile and laugh that husky little laugh that gave him too many ideas. But most of all he wanted her in his arms. And she would be, too. Soon. It was just going to take a little longer than he'd figured. But that was all right, too. He had never liked things or people easy. Challenges made the rewards that much more pleasurable.

"David?" Lacy said when he didn't answer.

"Are you sure you won't change your mind? The steaks are just dying for a grill, and I'm starving." He managed a teasing tone in spite of his not so teasing thoughts.

"I flatly refuse to attend a ball with bags under my eyes," she returned, borrowing a little of his humor. The temptation to agree was strong. But stronger still were deeply ingrained habits of her profession. She had work to do although she wished she didn't.

David exhaled deeply. "I know when I'm beaten. I'll see you tomorrow." He waited a second to see if she would change her mind. When there was only silence, he said goodbye and gently hung up the phone.

Lacy replaced the receiver absently, trying to understand herself. Since she had met David, the feeling of dissatisfaction that had been so faint that she had just begun to notice it was growing. Her career, the time-consuming, sometime puzzling and always challenging focus of her life, was no longer as clear-cut a goal as before. That bothered her, unsettled her and made her wish she dared talk to John about her feelings. But the way he was acting lately with regard to her personal life, or lack thereof, she was no longer certain she would get the answers she wanted, perhaps needed. She got to her feet and paced the room, feeling restless when just a moment before she had been content to sit and talk to David. She glanced at the briefcase stuffed with work and grimaced. She had to get Mann's financial statement read and get her paperwork up-to-date, plus go over the list of valuables the insurance companies had been kind enough to prepare on the victims. She didn't have time for this soul-searching. Sighing and frowning at the same time, she grabbed the case and stalked to the den.

Lacy cooked and ate dinner nose-deep in tangible assets. Her after-dinner soft drink was opened at the same time as Mann's financial statement. Her eyes widened as she scanned the pages of his monetary history. Ruined credit. Sarah's extended medical treatment had literally wiped the man out.

Sam's file showed only one color—clear, brilliant red. He owed money to everyone in town, not just the hospitals and the drug stores, but department stores, oil companies and loan organizations. Everyone! Most of his creditors carried *no further credit* notations beside their names. Lacy stared at the damning evidence, trying to figure out where it fit. It didn't, as far as she could see. If he had stolen anything where was the profit? Besides, he just didn't match the picture of the thief that was beginning to emerge. Sam was neither fit nor agile enough to pull the jobs. And he didn't seem to have the opportunity or the connections to be an inside man.

More questions. No answers. Lacy slipped into bed, trying to solve that puzzle and completely forgetting about David's unexpected invitation. She was almost comfortable with herself again, her personal life pushed aside for her profession. She was finally lost in the world she understood fully.

Saturday morning and most of the afternoon were spent on the streets, touching base with the small but effective group of informers that gave Lacy a pipeline to the less pleasant side of life. She wasn't fond of this portion of her work; in fact it was the one part she could cheerfully do without. Only the results made the exercise worthwhile. The first thing she did when she got home was to take a long, hot shower. She had less than two hours to turn herself into a woman beautiful enough to surprise David. Business had taken so long she'd had to cancel her hair appointment, and that only made her job that much more time-consuming. David rang the doorbell while she was putting the last touches on her makeup. She hurried to finish her eyes, not wanting to go to the door looking less than her best. She wanted him to see the complete picture, not some half-baked creation.

One quick glance in the mirror was all she had time for. The jade-green satin sheath was a perfect match for her eyes. The diamond-and-emerald pendant that John had given her on her twenty-first birthday and the matching earrings that had followed a year later were her only jewelry. Not that the gown needed much glitter. The ankle-to-thigh slit on the left side and the one-shoulder bodice held in place by crisscrossing strips of fabric was dramatically effective, a fact that was well noted by David when Lacy opened the door.

"Wow!" David stared at her for a full moment before he remembered he was still on the porch. "You look sensational. You make that dress."

Lacy smiled at his wording of the compliment. Pleased that all her searching through the stores and the rushing about this evening had had the desired effect, she said, "Most men would have said the dress made me." It was all she could do to just stand there. He looked like walking dynamite. The smile on his face teased her to join in his pleasure while promising things she hadn't experienced yet. Lacy felt a smile curve her own lips. Suddenly she felt young, excited and very feminine.

David shook his head, stepping forward to brush her lips with a kiss. "I'm neither blind nor a fool," he murmured huskily.

Lacy leaned into the kiss, enjoying the feel of his hands on her shoulders, the scent of him surrounding her. The temptation of deepening the kiss was irresistible. Her arms crept up to his neck as she softened against him. Seconds or minutes? Neither knew nor cared. David lifted his head, his breathing ragged.

"Wow!"

"Your vocabulary is severely limited," Lacy just managed to whisper, gazing at him through half-closed eyes. Her breath was a ragged sigh.

"If I weren't a gentleman, I would tell you all about something else that is severely limited." David pulled her tight against his chest. If he could have tucked her into his pocket he would have been happy. She was soft and sweet in his arms in a way that he had only imagined. His blood heated, making him wish these were still the days when a man could kidnap the woman he desired.

Lacy laughed softly, delighting in the strength of his hold. For so long she had been strong, and tomorrow she would be that way again. Her world demanded it. But for now she could relax, give when perhaps she could have taken. "Hello." In a way she felt as though she had just met herself and him.

"Hello to you, too," David returned with a grin. "You have two choices, a ball or a—"

Tipping her head, Lacy's smile widened. "Coward."

"No. Discreet."

Since they were standing hip to hip with only a few layers of fabric to conceal nature's inclination, there was precious little discretion. "Then I choose the ball. After all, we can't let those tickets of yours go to waste." One tiny part of her mind tried to insert the cool logic of her job. She ignored it. Right or wrong, she wanted this time with David for herself.

David released her reluctantly, looking absurdly disappointed. "I had a terrible feeling you would say that," he said, watching as she collected her wrap.

Lacy hesitated, wondering if there was hurt in his voice. She wanted to explain but didn't know how.

"First you refuse my wine and my steak, condemning me to eating alone, and now you refuse my advances."

She relaxed. His tone, if not his words, reassured her that he was teasing her. "Well, if at first you don't succeed..." She turned around in time to catch the sudden gleam of interest in his eyes.

A step forward brought him within touching distance. "Try, try again?"

"After the ball," she stated, hoping he would take her in his arms again. When he only grinned at her, she was disappointed. She tried to conceal a sigh, but he saw it anyway.

Running a finger down her cheek, he laughed softly. "I want to hold you, but if I do I promise we won't get to the dance. Perhaps we'd better forget about showing you my apartment and go straight to the ball." Before she could say a word he plucked the wrap from her hands and draped it around her shoulders. "Just remember you said 'after the ball.' I deserve some reward for eating alone last night."

With that kind of start Lacy could not help but enjoy her first taste of high society. Thanks to having David as an escort she had an entrée into the rarefied plane. The setting was nothing like Lacy expected. The decor was more ordinary than her own home. Yet looking at the people gathered about the room one could not help but recognize the wealth and influence of these old-moneyed families. It was in the cultured, almost accentless voices, the polished air of dignity, and attitude of command that surrounded each person present. An orchestra, not a band, played softly in the background. Dancers whirled about the floor with the grace and precision of professionals. The plumage of the ladies stood out boldly against the elegant austerity of their escorts. Lacy enjoyed it all, inhaling the atmosphere as one would a fine perfume. It was more habit and reflex that kept her on the alert to pick up any clues. Each face was matched with a name, some familiar through the media and others only through association with this company or that. Everyone appeared to belong. There were no servants with strange behavior, no suspicious whispers, no hushed-up conversations. Nothing. One big, fat zero as far as the robberies were concerned. In fact, she hadn't even heard them mentioned.

"What's that sigh for?" David asked as he drew her closer into his arms.

"Nothing. I was miles away in thought," Lacy murmured truthfully.

David controlled a grimace. Since they had arrived at the dance nothing had gone as he expected. In some strange way Lacy had slipped from his grasp. She danced with him, her body molded itself to his. She even smiled and talked to him, but he didn't have her total attention. That rankled, he discovered. Until tonight he had never known he had a possessive streak. He had never known he wanted all of the attention of the woman he held. It had been an effort of will not to hold her closer than this.

"Let's sit the rest of this one out." Ignoring the manners that had been drilled into him since birth, David didn't wait for her agreement before escorting her out the terrace doors. He couldn't wait another minute to know what was going on. He had to get some answers.

Lacy went with him. She had no real choice. The hold on her arm wasn't painful, but it was inescapable unless she wanted to make a scene. A short walk carried them to the concealment of the night shadows. Now she understood. He wanted to be alone with her. And she wanted that, too. Heat rose within her as the memory of the kiss they had shared returned. Her chin lifted, lashes drifted shut, lips parted, waiting...waiting...

"All right, Lacy, just what are you up to?" David demanded, not even noticing her provocative position.

Lacy's eyes opened with a snap, all thoughts of romance under the stars dying when she saw the anger on his face. His temper was more than she had experienced in a long time. He was clearly controlled, but there was a strength in him that warned her to tread carefully. The urge to take a backward step or two, or three was almost irresistible. Her chin lifted as she held her ground.

"I don't know what you mean."

David snorted. There was no other word for the sound that came from deep in his throat. "Tell me another one. I started the evening with a woman whom I thought was as attracted to me as I was to her. Or did I imagine that scene in your living room?" He peered at her in the darkness, wishing there was more light. He had a feeling she was hiding something.

"You didn't imagine it and you know it," Lacy responded before she thought. What had she done? What was he angry about?

"Okay, then why are you treating me like a piece of the furniture?"

"I am not," she denied reflexively. She searched her behavior, seeing nothing that could have sparked this kind of reaction. She suddenly realized what she had done. It had been so easy, so simple. It had started with seeing Emily Grayson. She had been looking around the room, searching for anything out of the ordinary. Clues? Suspicious people? How many of her dates accused her of this tunnel vision when she had slipped into this mode. And to do this to David. How could she!

"Oh," he drawled. "Then would you please explain to me why less than five minutes ago you agreed that anchovies and pickles on a strawberry sundae was your favorite dessert.''

"What!" Lacy demanded, staring at him. She couldn't have been that far-gone, could she? "I never did." She wanted to apologize but couldn't think how without telling him the whole truth.

"Believe me, you did," David returned grimly. "Now I want an explanation." He leaned against the railing of the veranda, crossing his ankles in a relaxed posture that wasn't relaxed at all. He would wait all night if he had to.

Lacy hesitated. She had to say something. Not to speak would only arouse more of his suspicions. Studying him, she tried to think of a reason. None came beyond the truth. She had to tell him. She wouldn't be compromising the case, so there was no real reason why she couldn't. "All right, David. I'll tell you, but not here," she murmured with a sigh.

His eyes narrowed at the flatness of her voice. The resignation in the usually lilting syllables was too obvious to miss. "Your place or mine?" For a moment he had the distinct and very uncomfortable feeling that something was seriously wrong. He shook his head, pushing the sensation away. His imagination must be stuck in overdrive.

Lacy sighed again, cursing her stupidity in mixing business with pleasure. She should have paid more attention to David or not given in to the temptation to kiss him. Even a rank amateur would have known she couldn't succumb to the sexual awareness she had for him one minute and treat him like a casual escort the next.

"Well?" David prompted, when she didn't reply.

"Your place is closer," she answered, finally. She could always call a taxi if he didn't want to take her home after he found out what she was doing. Occasionally, a

SHADOW WATCH   59

man was intimidated by her work. She didn't think David was one of those, but there was no way to be sure.

David pushed away from the railing and took her arm. Without a word he guided her through the beach club and out into the night. His car was brought to the front by the valet. In moments they were driving down the tree-lined main road toward the north tip of the Island. Lacy didn't try to break the silence. She was too busy trying to come up with a way to explain that wouldn't make it seem as though she was using him. For the first time in a long while she wondered about her motives and the demands her job made on her.

Four

———

All right. Let's have it."

Lacy walked deeper into the study, noticing without thinking about the rich colors of the room and the scent of the book-lined walls. There was an appealing aura of comfort and relaxation about the place. Unfortunately, it sat ill with the tension she and David had brought in with them. She hated lies and she hated what she had to tell David. Looking at her actions now she could see that, in a way, she had used him. Not consciously, it was true, but the results were the same.

"Mind if I sit down? It's been a long day." Without waiting for an answer she curled into one corner of the overstuffed couch and kicked off her shoes. Her actions were more to give herself time to think than to imply a nonchalance she was far from feeling. Taking a deep breath, she looked at her unwilling host. The expression in his eyes said that he couldn't believe her actions.

"I wish you wouldn't do that," David muttered, stalking across the room to throw himself down in the chair opposite her.

"Do what?"

"Act like none of this is affecting you. You're the only person I have ever seen who can go through the motions of living without it showing in your behavior. The only place that is a true mirror of what you're thinking is in your eyes, and then only if one looks very closely and very quickly, for even there you hide yourself away."

Lacy blinked. "You're very perceptive," she murmured, watching him as closely as he watched her.

"I have a feeling I'll need to be before this night is over."

"I'm sorry." Lacy shook her head, disgusted with herself for blurting out the apology.

One brow kicked upward in surprise. "For what?"

"For using you." There was no other way to say it so Lacy didn't try. She expected a reaction but she didn't get it. David's expression didn't change by so much as a flicker of an eyelash. If he thought her good at emotional stonewalling, he was better.

"How?"

"I'm a private investigator for the Tipton Detective Agency." First blankness, then comprehension, slipped subtly across David's features. If Lacy hadn't been looking for his reaction she would have missed it entirely.

"So?"

Sighing, Lacy realized he wasn't going to make it easy for her. But then why should he? He was entitled to his piece of her hide. She hadn't treated him fairly at all.

"I'm working on the robberies, Grayson and Osgood."

"What does that have to do with me? Am I suspect?"
The sarcasm in his voice was plain.

"No."

"Why not? I thought the police had no leads. I've even
heard rumors that it was an inside operation. What could
be more inside than being a resident of the Island and
knowing the people as friends? Plus, I am an architect. I
design buildings, Graysons' to be specific. I could have
gotten my hands on the plans for the security system if I
had wanted to."

David pushed her, knowing but not caring that he was
being unfair. His pride was smarting, his libido shot, and
more than that he was hurt. The first two he could understand even if he was unfamiliar with the responses.
The third was a complete shock. More than the others,
it made him want to force her to feel the same betrayal he
knew. The second he realized his motives, he stopped the
outpouring of angry words, but not before the damage
was done.

Lacy's eyes shone with green fire as she stiffened on the
couch. If it hadn't been David, if she hadn't been feeling
so guilty she might have been able to hold onto her temper. "I know you aren't a suspect because you've been
checked out. As has everyone else on this island of
money. Do you want me to quote book and verse of your
financial statement?" She lifted a hand and began tick-
ing off the facts of his life. "Parents, money and background from the year one. Two brothers, one in politics,
slated to be the next senator from Maryland. The other
is a criminal lawyer who specializes in cases involving
high-visibility crime figures. History is solidly pro government and just as solidly against corruption, crime and
anything else that smacks of dishonesty. Marsh Archi-
tecture. Small firm specializing in reviving interest in and

building of Addison Mizner type homes. You have enough money so that you could be a jet-setter with gold-plated tastes and still never run through it all. Instead you work, damn hard by all accounts.''

"Suspect?" She laughed once, almost grimly. "Hardly. The only thing anyone could suspect you of is liking the ladies, but even that's in moderation and apparently not more than one at a time." She hadn't liked reading that little tidbit in his file. In many ways that one paragraph on his private life had been responsible for the dress she now wore. She hadn't wanted to be just one of his companions. She had wanted him to see her as something more. And he did, all right. She was the woman who had used him and by omission lied to him.

David glared at her, hating the recounting, especially the last part. "I suppose if I asked for the figures of my checkbook you could give me those too?"

"I could." She couldn't back down from the condemnation she saw in his eyes. The research the firm had done was necessary for the case of the moment as well as for her safety. Although where David was concerned her safety wasn't a major consideration.

"You've got your nerve," David exploded, coming off the chair to pace to the window, then back. He stopped before her, glaring down at her. The way she stared right back at him angered him almost as much as her prying had done. "You aren't even sorry, are you?"

Lacy shook her head. "Not about checking you out. That had to be done. But I am sorry about not telling you who I was earlier. I don't have one excuse for it that would even make sense." She spread her hands, her temper dying as quickly as it had come. "I can only say I'm sorry."

"You used me."

"I know," she agreed quietly.

David couldn't believe she could sit there and look him straight in the eye even with an apology. Yet she did it. Her hands were folded in her lap, her head up, her gaze steady. Anger might be clawing at his insides, but she seemed as calm as a tidal pool. Or did she? There was something in her eyes. He took a step closer, trying to force back the anger and hurt enough to study what was almost hidden from him.

"And the kiss? Was that just window dressing?"

"Did it feel like window dressing?" she countered, needing his reassurance almost as much as she needed his forgiveness, things she had never before asked of anyone.

David's hands clenched at his sides. Emotion won the battle against logic and the beginnings of his feelings for her. If he had known her longer, if there had been more between them than a kiss, he might have tempered his anger, his hurt.

"Damn you. Why me?"

"Because you had the tickets. Because you asked me to go. Because I wanted to see you again." Lacy's life dealt more in subterfuge and evasion than truth. But she believed passionately in honesty. Because of that belief and the pain she could sense in him, she gave him a weapon if he chose to use it. She gave him the whole truth, risking being hurt by him in return.

David stared at her, unable to comprehend the last of her admissions. It had been said in the same flat tone as the others, yet it stood out as though Lacy had shouted the words.

"You're lying. I was just a means to an end."

"I don't lie. If I can help it." She wanted to crawl away somewhere and lick her wounds. There was no mercy in him right now. He couldn't see her side. "I can't make you believe me. Only you can decide if I'm telling you the truth."

David didn't know what to think. Lacy was outside his experience. She couldn't be a user. For a long moment he just looked at her. Still she didn't look away.

"And now?" The question was drawn from him against his will.

"That's up to you." She ached to hear him say they could start again without the lies.

"How?"

She hesitated, wanting to tell him her side of it first. But she didn't have the nerve. Lacy Tipton didn't have the nerve to tell one man she wanted him, needed him to want her. So she chose familiar paths, paths she understood, paths that did not threaten her way of life. If he couldn't accept her, maybe he could accept helping her find the thief that lurked in the shadows of the Island.

"I need to approach this case from a different angle. The police, Garrick Security and the agency have gone over everything. Nothing. The thief is good. So are we. But we're missing something. I'm going to try coming at the problem from the inside out. You could be the key to the lock."

David drew back, his breath emerging in an angry hiss. "Are you suggesting I should spy on my friends, on people I have known for years?"

"I am suggesting you help me to protect them," Lacy came back sharply. So far, she had allowed David to vent his justifiable anger without check. Calling her a spy by inference slipped under her guard and prodded her temper.

"That's ridiculous and you know it. So try the real words, not some slick evasion."

"I need your help." Lacy rose to face him. "There, is that real enough to suit you?"

"I don't think I've ever met anyone less needing of help than you," he snapped, stalking for his desk. "I'm calling you a cab. I'm sure you'll understand if I don't see you home."

Lacy stared at his stiff back, wondering which emotion was uppermost in her mind. He was tossing her out without a qualm. He was throwing away a chance to help, and he was slashing at her, determined to pay her back for using him. Each action generated feelings too strong to be given free rein. Once started, she had a feeling she wouldn't stop until she had released every bit of temper coiling tighter with each second.

The slamming of the receiver back in the cradle caught her attention. "The butler will show you out."

She had to try one more time. "Won't you at least think about helping out? You have a stake in this too. Don't you see?"

"By doing what? Listening to you? Peeking around keyholes? I'm an architect, remember. You're the private detective here. You can handle evasions and lies. I won't."

Lacy took each damning word as a body blow. She flinched with each stinging lash, but dodged none. Where there had been emotion, now there was only cold silence. Guilt rode her. Pain tore at her. It shouldn't have hurt this much. The words echoed in the emptiness of her mind. Pride was the only thing she had left, and even it was battered and frayed.

"I have feelings, too many sometimes. I hurt for the people who are prey to humanity's cruelties. I see things, too. Things you, in your ivory tower, read about but don't know. I hear worse than you can throw at me. I've held a dying man in my arms and watched his blood run like a river from a knife wound. I closed his eyes when he couldn't see the sun overhead any longer.''

David took a step toward her, drawn against his will by the agony that shone briefly in her eyes. She turned away to pick up her purse, missing the hand he half lifted to her.

"I'll wait in the foyer so I won't contaminate your world with my sordid presence."

Before he could stop her she was gone, the door closing silently behind her. David stood there, unable to move. His temper had made him label her unfeeling. He had known that was a lie the moment after he had uttered the damning words. He should have called them back, but he hadn't. He could not forgive the method by which she had involved him in her work. Had he been given a choice it would have been different. But she had used him and that he had to remember. The memory of her eyes, the stark pain he had seen, stayed with him too. Her face had been calm, yet her hands had gripped together as though to impart strength or warmth. Lacy Tipton was definitely a woman unlike any he had ever known. She was capable and strong when she had to be, yet soft in his arms. She held pain hidden in her eyes and, he suspected, in her heart. She did a job many men would not tackle and still remained feminine. And, damn her, she intrigued him, he admitted silently even as he turned away from the door separating them. Better she should go back to her world than to invade his.

Lacy left the house as soon as she heard the cab pull into the drive. Weariness seeped from every pore when she settled back in the seat and gave the driver her address. The whole day had been nothing but a series of dead ends. And then the dance. That had been disaster, a fact she would have to report to John as soon as she got home. And David? Her mind shied from his name. His words had touched too many nerves. She should have known better than to try to steal a few moments of pleasure for herself by keeping what she did from him. No one liked to be used, with or without cause. Her needs had taken what looked like the only chance she had to legitimately insert herself into the Island clan. John would not be pleased at her bungling.

And he wasn't. "Of all the dumb things to do," John muttered, his exasperation clear even through the phone lines.

"I said I was wrong," Lacy reminded him.

"That isn't much help at this stage of the game. Why did you do it?" he demanded. "It's not like you to be so clumsy."

Lacy closed her eyes, feeling an unaccustomed sting of tears. Damn, she never cried. And she wouldn't now. "I'm sick of nearly every man I meet thinking he needs to prove himself. Not one of them sees my work as just a job. Because I can handle myself physically, speak the two languages of this bilingual state and have a master's in criminology, you would think I was personally threatening their egos. Just once I wanted to enjoy one evening without dealing with that."

"Why the devil did you think David Marsh would be worried about your work? From what you told me of his file I'd think he could handle it, and you if you had been honest." The exasperation was combined with certainty.

Lacy pressed her fingers to her temple trying to soothe away a headache that was growing worse by the second. Briefly, she wondered how stupid one woman could be in a twenty-four hour period. John didn't suffer fools gladly or easily. "All I can say is, I'm sorry I botched it."

The weariness in her voice startled him. Lacy and he had had words before without her sounding this defeated. John swore once, an oath that he would normally never have used around Lacy. "Honey, are you all right? You don't sound like yourself," he said gruffly. "Is there something about this you're holding back? Would it help if I talked to him? I could tell him it was my idea that you keep your occupation under wraps until after the dance."

She had brought this on herself. She wouldn't allow John to be her scapegoat. "Thanks for the offer, but no. I've already told him why I did it and that it was my own idea. I won't lie about my motives now. It was bad enough I involved him at all."

John didn't say anything for a moment. He knew Lacy's pride as well as he knew his own. If their positions had been reversed he wouldn't have wanted someone taking his flack either. "How angry was he?" But, on the other hand, he didn't want her being torn up over something that, while it was an error in judgement, was necessary for the job at hand.

"Very."

"He didn't hurt you, did he?"

Lacy almost laughed at the careful question. There were far greater hurts than physical ones. "No, he didn't hurt me," she replied untruthfully. She felt no remorse at this lie.

John opened his mouth to probe further, then just as quickly closed it again. That flat tone was one he knew well. Lacy had a reserve to her that even he could not penetrate. "What's next? Did you pick up any leads?"

Lacy relaxed slightly with the return to business. She'd been afraid John would push for more information. "Not yet. But my snitches are on the street. If an ant moves out there I'll hear about it eventually."

"Eventually is what worries me," John muttered irritably.

"I know. This guy is too smart for words. Two robberies in a few weeks. If he stays on schedule we'll be hearing from him again soon."

"Don't remind me. Garrick has been on my neck all day. The man is going to go up in smoke before this is over."

"I may join him if I don't get a break soon."

John's fervent agreement was rough. "Got any more to tell me?"

"I wish I did."

"Then get some sleep. You sound bushed."

"Yes, Uncle-daddy," Lacy said, using the nickname she had given him the first year she had come to him. The smile was in his voice as he came back with his own title for her.

"Brat!"

They hung up the phones together, neither needing nor wanting a more affectionate display. Lacy stared out the window, thinking of nothing. She was past being tired. Discouragement and hurt were bitter pills and ones she hated taking. Sleep was long in coming. A warm shower didn't help. Neither did a glass of brandy. She was almost relieved when the phone rang at one in the morning. The sound of John's voice brought her upright with a jerk, her hand fumbling for the lamp beside the bed.

"The Dellwood house was robbed tonight," John announced tersely. "Riley just called me. Get over there as soon as you can. Here's the address."

Lacy didn't bother with a pencil although it and a pad were on the nightstand beside her. Instead, she pulled off her gown, tossing it at the chair. "Twenty minutes at the outside," she said abruptly before hanging up the phone.

Jeans and a lightweight pullover sweater were yanked on as she grabbed her jogging shoes, brush and handbag. In less than three minutes she was running down the stairs to the front door. Traffic was minimal, and she made all the lights between her town house and the Island. It was hard to drive one-handed and put on shoes at the same time, but she managed. Brushing her hair was slightly easier and accomplished only seconds before she pulled into the Dellwood's driveway. The parking area was filled with two police cars, the Dellwood's Rolls and another vehicle she could have sworn was David's. Lights blazed out of every window. The butler answered the door at her first knock. If she hadn't known there had been a crime committed on the premises she would never have guessed from the man's unruffled demeanor. It was only when she entered the living room and saw the various people milling about that the scene took on any life.

A pair of older ladies, still dressed in evening gowns and a ransom in jewels, occupied the sofa. Chief Riley and another man were questioning both. The doors to the terrace that overlooked the intracoastal were thrown open, and Lacy could hear voices coming from outside. No one noticed her. No one, that was, but the man who came into the room a few seconds after she did.

"So they called you already," David muttered from behind her. His emotions were still seesawing over this woman. One moment he wanted to say the words that would let her off the hook, and the next he wanted to shake her for what she had done to him.

Lacy swung around to find him glaring at her as though the whole situation was her fault. "Did you have an objection?" she asked sharply, before she thought. "What are you doing here?"

"I'm here because I was called. And whether I have an objection or not is a moot point."

Lacy allowed the second half of his statement to pass unchallenged. She focused on the first and tried to forget everything else that had passed between them. It wasn't easy. In fact, it was close to impossible when he kept watching her without speaking. Nothing of the man who had teased her with laughter, who had kissed her with passion, lingered on his face or in the way he watched her.

"Are you a relative or something?" She had to speak if for no other reason than to break the silence between them.

"Or something."

Exhaling slowly, Lacy tried to remember all the reasons to be polite to the victims and families of the victims when at the scene of a crime. "Be specific, please." This time she would stay well within the bounds of her profession.

David opened his mouth, intending to be just as unhelpful as possible when he heard his godmother begin to cry. Two steps took him from Lacy's side to the sofa. He leveled Riley with a glare. "Don't you think you have asked enough questions for tonight?" He sat down, taking the older of the women in his arms. "They don't know anything."

"We have to finish," the chief began patiently.

Lacy laid a hand on Riley's shoulder. "May I help?" she asked softly. She and Riley had established a mutual respect when they had met. Both knew that sometimes a woman's lighter touch accomplished more in these circumstances.

David lifted his head to glare at her. Only out of consideration for the shock his godmother and her sister had been through did he keep from expressing his opinion of Lacy's interference. It was bad enough to have to sit through the questioning of Clara and Alicia, something that was necessary for the police report. Having Lacy retrace barren ground was more than he could stomach.

Chief Riley got up with a sigh. "Would you try? We've managed to get a list, complete we think, of what was taken. What we can't get is the correct time they returned home or exactly what, if anything, alerted them to the robbery. They had both gone upstairs and then come down to check the house. That's when they discovered the doors to the terrace open. The thief could have still been here."

"Oh mercy," Alicia whimpered, pressing a delicate handkerchief to her lips. "We never thought of that."

Lacy took Riley's chair. "Most people don't," she murmured soothingly, reaching out to take the other woman's hand. David had his arms full of one sister, but the other needed consoling too. "I think you both did admirably. I'm not sure I would have been brave enough to come down those stairs because I heard a sound that made me curious."

"Oh, but it wasn't a sound." Clara lifted her head from David's shoulder. "We never got upstairs."

Alicia nodded. "She's right. We were halfway up when we realized that there was draft coming from the living room."

Riley spoke up. "I thought you said you went up to your bedroom."

"Did we?" The women exchanged a confused look.

Lacy ignored Riley's barely controlled grunt of exasperation. "So you felt a draft from the living room. Then what?"

"We went to check," Clara answered.

"Did you see anything unusual?"

Clara shook her head. Lacy turned to Alicia, who spoke. "I thought I saw something by the window. Do you remember, Clara dear?"

"So you did. But it was only a shadow. We looked."

David stared at the two women that he had known all of his life, suddenly realizing that they could have been seriously hurt. The more they said, the stronger the possibility became that the robber had been inside the house when they had come home. His arms tightened on the frail body he held. His eyes lifted to Lacy's face, catching the sympathy and gentleness in her expression as she posed another question for Clara. There was nothing in her voice to denote more than casual interest, unlike the barely restrained urgency with which Riley had asked his questions. Lacy could have been hosting a tea she was so relaxed. And because of her attitude he could feel the tension sliding from Clara's body and see it also leave Alicia. In that moment he realized again how wrong he had been about Lacy.

Anger flowed from him as interest and curiosity took over. Now he watched her to learn, to understand. She handled the rest of the interview with caring and delicacy, but somehow she extracted information that neither Riley nor he had been able to obtain. And when she was done both Clara and Alicia were visibly less upset than they had been.

"My dear, you will find our things, will you not?" Clara leaned forward to touch Lacy's hand.

Lacy smiled gently. "I'll give it my best shot," she replied. "So far I don't think the thief has disposed of any of his booty. If we're lucky, he won't until the furor dies down. By that time maybe the chief will have caught up with him." Lacy rose, closing her notebook. "Now if you will excuse me I think I'll take a look around outside."

Clara and Alicia got to their feet. "Feel free, my dear." The men might not have been in the room for all the attention the ladies paid to them. "It is past our bedtime." Clara turned and patted David's cheek. "Be sure our guest has a nightcap before she goes home, dear." With that the ladies left the room arm in arm, much to the astonishment of their audience.

"Well, I'll be," Riley muttered, staring after them.

David silently seconded his words. He turned to ask Lacy what magic she had worked only to find her gone. Reacting instinctively, he followed her outside. Despite the many lights on the exterior of the building it wasn't long before he was swallowed up by the night. There was no moon, no light beyond the golden pool about the house itself to show the way. Only his familiarity with the property kept him on the path that led to the water's edge. He stopped, seeing nothing, no shadows moving, no sounds to alert him of another's presence.

"Lacy?" he called softly, cursing himself as a fool for not having brought a flashlight. He had thought the police would still be out here checking for clues. "Lacy," he repeated when there was no answer. Had she left already, he wondered, scanning the inky night.

"Yes."

The soft answer spoken just behind him and to the left startled him. He swung around and there she was, a shadow of deeper darkness than those around him. He could barely see her face. Her voice was little more than a whisper.

"I'm sorry," he murmured, the words slipping from him without thought.

"For what?" She asked because she had to. She had to know how complete his forgiveness was.

"For what I said earlier."

Lacy tipped her head, trying to understand. David was different than he had been when she arrived. Something had happened to change his opinion of her, but she couldn't think what it could be. If anything, her actions this night should have reinforced his beliefs. She had virtually ignored him for most of the evening, and she had certainly used the rapport she had established with Riley to get her questions answered. David was too intelligent not to know that.

"I don't understand," she admitted finally.

"Neither do I. But I want to." He paused then added, "And if the offer is still open I'd like to see you again. Help, too, if I can."

Five

———

Lacy didn't say anything for a moment. She honestly had to admit it had occurred to her that David would change his mind now the thief had victimized one of his family. Most people felt outraged and in the mood for retaliation when they were in similar situations. From a professional point of view she was glad he had reconsidered. From a personal one she was a bit disappointed that it had been the thief who had prompted the reversal. Stifling the latter emotion wasn't easy, but she tried. She had already seen the error of mixing business and pleasure with this man. She wouldn't be a fool twice.

"Did you hear me?" David asked when she didn't answer.

"I heard. My question is why."

"What do you mean, why?"

Lacy took a step closer. "Don't be obtuse. A few hours ago you accused me of trying to recruit you to spy on your friends. What's changed between then and now?"

David moved nearer. "What's changed is my godmother's life," he replied, not understanding the question.

"Then the answer is no. The last thing I need is some vigilante-type after the bad guy. This isn't the movies."

David drew back, unable to believe she was refusing him. "Just exactly what does that mean?" he snapped, feeling anger lick at the edges of his mind. Normally he was a very even-tempered man, but around Lacy his control was almost nonexistent.

"It means that we aren't here to avenge your godmother. All we want is to catch a thief. You aren't detached enough to be any help. The first time we get a glimpse of the man who might be the culprit you'll be all over him like a case of heat rash. None of us, not me, not Tipton's, nor Garrick's, nor the police can afford that," she stated flatly, calling the situation as experience had taught her to see it.

David's jaw clenched tight against the words aching for expression. "I am not stupid," he managed grittily.

Lacy sighed. "I never said you were." She hadn't meant to make him angry. "I know this is going to sound hard, but the law is the arbitrator here. Not you. Not me. There is a crook out there, picking his time and his victim. We don't want to just catch him; we want to stop him, and that means getting a conviction when he goes to trial. One slip and a defense attorney gets the guy off. I don't want that. And you don't, either." Lacy could understand how David felt. If the positions were reversed she'd feel the same.

But she really needed David's help. Having an entrée into the social scene of the Island wouldn't have been necessary at all if the residents weren't so bent on protecting their privacy. With the absence of clues, she desperately needed a way to move freely among them. David was the only ticket that had come to hand. And now he was more out of reach than ever: she couldn't afford a self-appointed sheriff. She wanted this thief caught and convicted.

David digested her words, finding the sense and logic in them. Stifling his outrage and anger, he suggested, "Show me what to do and I'll do it." He could see in her expression that she didn't believe him. His control slipped a notch.

If he couldn't reach her with reason then he would appeal to the feminine side of her nature. One more step brought him close enough to reach out and touch her. She didn't move away as his hand curled around her upper arm. He felt her tense. He didn't like that stiffening. His temper had lost him the softness in her. Her feminine side was in hiding, leaving behind only the detective. In that second he realized he wouldn't do his cause any good this way. Unconsciously, his fingers tightened in denial of what his mind told him.

Lacy was too caught up in her thoughts to be more than marginally aware of his touch. Instead, she was weighing the needs of the job versus the risk. A small nod of decision was slow to come. She wasn't sure she could hold onto her emotions with David around, and because of the job, because of the words they had spoken, she had to be careful. "Do I have your word that you won't do anything without checking with me first?" She peered up at him.

David didn't hesitate, not about this. She was the expert here. "You have my word."

"All right," she agreed slowly, still not too certain his involvement was worth the risk to the case or her peace of mind. "Let's go back up to the house." She hesitated, then continued resolutely. This time there would be no omissions of information. "We will have to act—" she paused, searching for a word "—affectionate," she decided, settling for the least demanding of the descriptions she could have chosen.

David almost smiled in the darkness, hearing the catch of uncertainty in her voice. Lacy wasn't nearly as calm and professional as she pretended. Satisfaction and pleasure that he disturbed her weren't exactly the most admirable of reactions, but he couldn't help feeling them. When she allowed his hold on her to remain, and even brushed against him in such a way that he had to slide his hand down and catch her wrist or let her go, he smiled faintly. For a moment he forgot the theft and savored recapturing a bit of what he had lost.

"Very good," Lacy murmured quietly, needing to say something to disrupt the intimacy of the silent darkness. She shivered slightly at the touch of his body against hers. Being affected by David was not something she dared tolerate.

David felt like throwing her hand away at the good-boy tone she used even though he suspected why she had spoken. He had felt her faint response. "We'll have to be a lot more...affectionate than this, you know." He felt, rather than saw her shrug. The now familiar, offhand gesture bothered him a lot until he remembered the tremor she had tried to hide.

"Perhaps," Lacy replied, not even sure herself why she hadn't spelled out what she would require of him in the next few days. She could have said that there wasn't enough privacy to allow her to lay out her strategy. She could have said there would be time enough tomorrow. What she wouldn't have said was that she wanted a little of her own back for the hurtful words he had said earlier in the evening. Her actions weren't admirable, but at the moment she didn't care. That was what bothered her. She was demanding David put his feelings aside when she hadn't done the same herself.

Stopping abruptly, she said, "I'm sorry. That was unnecessary and uncalled-for. I was trying to punish you for tonight."

They were near the house so the exterior lights now touched them. Both could see clearly. David studied her face, seeing the woman and not the detective. "I think it was called for," he whispered slowly, lifting his free hand to lightly stroke her cheek. This side of her he could understand and relate to. "I hurt you earlier without cause. It is I who should be asking forgiveness. I still stand by what I said about using me. I'll even admit I was hurt. I wanted you to want to be with me because you wanted it, too. It never occurred to me that there could be another reason." He laughed shortly, almost grimly. "That was my ego talking."

Lacy hadn't expected his honesty. Most men she knew would have crawled in a hole in the ground before admitting such things. Truth begets truth. Suddenly, she didn't want him to be the only one with enough courage to be vulnerable.

"It wasn't just the job," she confessed, watching him closely. "Although it should have been. And because it wasn't is the real reason I kept who I was a secret."

David frowned. "I don't understand."

"Ms. Tipton?"

The call from the terrace interrupted whatever Lacy would have said. Both she and David turned in the direction of the light to find Chief Riley heading toward them. Shrewd eyes flickered over the familiarity of their position. Lacy could see the sudden understanding in the older man's expression. By now he would know that she and David had attended the dance together. The conclusions he would draw were exactly the image Lacy wanted to project. Lacy risked a sidelong glance beneath her lashes. The knowledge of the chief's assumptions was in the look David gave her. She sighed soundlessly. Another lie.

"My men and I are leaving now. Is there anything else you need from us tonight?"

Lacy shook her head, without widening the distance between her and David. "No. I'll stop by early tomorrow to check the results of the fingerprinting."

Riley inclined his head, then took his leave.

David watched him go. "How far are we supposed to go with this charade?"

"Not here," Lacy murmured, turning to him. "Sound carries at night, remember." She reached up and touched his cheek, using the caress for an excuse to step nearer.

David took his cue, trying not to lose himself in the fantasy of the way she moved against him. This wasn't real. Bending his head he brought his lips close to her ear. "Then where?"

"My house. Tonight, if you can leave your godmother."

Lacy had her own problems remembering the role she intended to play. David's warm breath against her neck sent delicious shivers down her spine. It would have been easy to forget that they were acting.

"Let me check on her and then we can go," David said. He had meant to give them a little time. Then she turned to him, softening in his arms. Her scent wrapped around him, tempting him. His lips found the delicate swirls of her ear and traced the curves. A tiny nip on the lobe and then a slow journey down the side of her neck to end in a kiss at the base of her throat.

Lacy inhaled sharply at the unexpected caress, but nothing could have made her move away. This was only a part of what she had wanted from him earlier. Was it so wrong to take it now when it was offered, she asked herself even as she leaned into his touch. They were hurting no one. In fact his actions, if seen, would only lend credence to their budding relationship.

He lifted his head, seeing the same desire in her eyes that he knew burned in his. "I want you." The words were stark, spoken without intent to seduce or even convince. Simple truth, unadorned by the experience he had in abundance.

"Tell me something I don't know," Lacy suggested, frustrated with herself and the situation. Her rules of noninvolvement were strained to the limit, and all he had done was kiss her.

David lifted his head, recognizing the emotion behind the flippant words. He opened his lips to demand an explanation, then realized now was not the moment. Yet the thought of waiting irritated him. He had a feeling that Lacy would use the time it took to reach her place to slip into the detective mode that was so impossible to breach. He didn't want that. He wanted her soft and yielding in his arms. He wanted to feel her move against him, to make the act real.

Lacy covered his hands, silently asking for her release. David gave it, slowly, his eyes intent on her. "I'll go ahead. You follow when you can."

David nodded before taking her hand in his. "For the act," he murmured as her brows raised in surprise. "You never know who could be watching."

Lacy entered her town house for the second time that night. She kicked off her shoes and headed straight for the kitchen. The need of coffee and something to eat was reaching desperate proportions. It only took a minute to ready the coffee maker and to raid the freezer for some frozen pastries.

"Thank heavens for microwave ovens," she mumbled as she inserted a cinnamon bun on a tray and punched in the appropriate numbers. In a few seconds the scent of fresh-baked goods filled the house. Lacy poured herself a cup of coffee as soon as it was ready and lifted the pastry, now cooled, to her lips. She managed to finish the bun before the doorbell rang, announcing David's arrival. Mug in hand, she padded to the door to let him in.

"How did you know I needed coffee?" David plucked the cup from her hold, and turning it, drank from the same place as she had.

Lacy inhaled sharply at the provocative action. She could almost feel his lips on hers, feel the light lick of his tongue as he wiped the last drop from the rim. Her eyes met his. She could see the memory of their kisses, their depths and the promise of the future she had to ignore.

"That's mine," she grumbled, taking back her cup. She used words to provide camouflage. If she had been thinking she would have realized how clearly her needs were shown in her defenses.

"Okay, where's mine?" David closed the door and then followed his nose to the kitchen. The pot of coffee on the stand made his eyes widen in pleasure. Without waiting for an invitation he poured himself a cup. "Where's the sugar?"

Lacy watched him move about the room as though he belonged there. At least he seemed familiar with the environment, which was more than she could say for herself. "I don't use it." Actually, she did, but she had forgotten where she had put the stuff the last time she had gone grocery shopping. Rather than search for it she had decided to take her brew black.

"Well, I do." David opened the overhead cabinet nearest him. A tumble of paper goods showered down. He jumped back, spilling the contents of the mug he held.

Lacy viewed the mess with the resignation born of experience. Hardly hearing his apology, she reached for the mop she always kept at hand. "You made it; you mop it up."

David eyed the implement, then her. It was a challenge, pure and simple. "I'm not very good at this," he warned her, issuing the understatement of the year without a blink.

Lacy grinned, enjoying his obvious lack of knowledge. One of her less admirable characteristics was liking to discover others in the world who were as inept as she around the house. "Neatness counts," she murmured wickedly.

David glared down at the mess he had made.

"It won't go away just because you want it to."

"I know that," he muttered, realizing he was stuck. The fact that Lacy was enjoying every bit of his discomfort only added to the problem. How hard could cleaning be, he wondered, as he gingerly took the mop and plopped it right in the middle of the brown puddle of coffee. Seconds later he was staring at splatters of mud-colored water on his pale gray jeans. An oath escaped before he could stop it. "These are brand new."

Lacy laughed. She couldn't help it. How many times had she splattered her panty hose until she realized one did not slap a dry mop on a spill without taking a bath in the process.

David gave her a look that promised retribution. She ignored it, and him, to pick up the paper products and stuff them willy-nilly back in the cabinet.

"If you would try a little organization . . ." David began.

"I suppose every thing has its own place in your house," she murmured, before he could begin on the lecture in neatness she had heard a hundred times from John.

David watched her for a moment, seeing something he hadn't realized. She felt awkward, off balance about the mess in her cabinets. He wasn't exactly certain why, but he could tell she was hurting or had been hurt. "Not everyone is a neatness freak. In fact, there are those of us who probably carry it to extremes."

Lacy blinked, not having expected his perception. Giving herself time to think she leaned against the counter, her legs crossed at the ankles. She took a sip of coffee before agreeing, "True."

David finished cleaning, set the mop aside and picked up his coffee again. He lifted his own mug to his lips, swallowed, then lowered it enough to watch her over the rim. It was time to change the subject. Lacy was looking as wary and troubled as the first time he had seen her. "I should have waited for an invitation before I invaded your kitchen."

Lacy gave a small nod. "True." Then she smiled, relaxing a little. "Something about a night like this one tends to eliminate barriers that usually only fall with time."

"Is that why I feel as though we can skip a few steps in getting to know each other?" His gaze held hers, waiting for her reaction. Her lashes were heavy with fatigue, making him wish he had the right to send her to bed instead of staying here carrying on a nonsensical conversation. He wanted to see that smile again.

"We have skipped a few steps. The point to remember is that this isn't real."

David stilled for an instant. He had been right. She had used the time they were apart to slip away from him. "It can be. You said you wanted to be with me tonight," he reminded her carefully.

Lacy met his eyes, not backing down from the challenge. "I also said I made a mistake."

"I don't agree."

"You don't have to." She hesitated. She didn't want to recall him to his promise. But she would to get the job done.

"You're afraid that if we get involved the case or assignment or whatever you call it will suffer?"

"Yes." She sighed, rubbing her temple lightly.

He didn't like that. Had she had the same experience with some other man somewhere in her past? He wanted to ask but didn't dare.

"Aren't you forgetting something?"

"Such as?"

"We're both adults and supposedly have control of our passions."

Lacy just managed not to choke on her drink. If the kiss they had shared earlier was control she didn't want to see no control. She couldn't point that out, however, without emphasizing how affected she'd been. So she evaded. "I'm not into light affairs. Tried it once when I was much younger and hated it," she added candidly.

David scowled. "I don't recall proposing a light affair."

"What then?"

Backed into a corner, David took the only course open to him: honesty. "Lacy, you ask the damnedest questions. How the devil do I know where we'll end up? I'm an architect, not a fortune-teller. All I'm suggesting is that we get to know each other better."

"In other words, let nature take its course."

He inclined his head, wishing he had never started the conversation. "Do you always need everything up front?" he asked, before he thought.

"Always. Questions make me curious to know the answers. I don't like loose ends."

"I think I resent being termed a loose end."

"There are worse descriptions," Lacy returned in the same dry tone.

Deciding he had pushed her as far as he dared for the moment, he held out his hand. She had opened to him a little. He wanted to keep her aware, not send her into hiding again. "Pact?"

Lacy looked at his hand, then at him. "Pact." She placed her hand in his, feeling the warmth of his grip close carefully around her fingers. "Now can we talk about the next few days?"

"That's why I'm here," he said, drawing her out of the kitchen toward the living room. "But let's get comfortable first."

Lacy let him push her gently down on the couch, but she almost jumped up when he lifted her feet to rest on the low table in front of it. When a pillow was tucked beneath her head, she just stared. "What are you doing?"

"You're tired. I assume you will be running all day tomorrow and on precious little, if any, sleep. I'm helping you relax while you command your pet how best to serve you."

Lacy all but gaped at him. Anyone or anything less like a pet than David she had yet to see. She had a feeling he was doing all the leading and she was following. "You're nuts," she stated succinctly.

"No." He took a seat on the end of the couch. "Only trying to get you to smile again," he explained, completely serious. "You worry too much." He leaned across and touched the furrows on her brows with a gentle finger. "And right now I think you've either got a headache or are getting one. That's the third time since I arrived that you've starting massaging your temples."

Dropping her hand from where she had, indeed, been trying to soothe away a dull throb, Lacy stared at him. She wasn't accustomed to people being so perceptive where she was concerned. It was always she who saw what others did not. And it had been a long time since anyone had tried taking care of her.

"I don't need a mother," she murmured.

She noted the lack of firmness in her voice with amazement. If anyone else, including John, had taken over the way David was doing she would have been irritated to say the least. It was odd she had no such reaction to David. In fact, if she was being honest, she had to admit it felt kind of nice to have someone worrying over her. She was weary of being strong and self-sufficient all the time.

David ignored her words because to say anything would be to say too much. It was patently obvious that Lacy took care of Lacy without anyone's help. It was also clear that in her life her career held first place. He had never been in a home that looked less lived-in than hers. If it hadn't been for the smell of coffee that had emanated from the kitchen when he had arrived he would have sworn she had never set foot inside that room at all.

"Okay, now tell me what you want me to do to help," he suggested, putting the puzzle of Lacy away for the moment. Working with her had gained him the time he needed to learn about this intriguing woman and he meant to use it. But right now he needed to learn about the job they would do.

Lacy was glad to focus on the case. Trying to figure David out was making her distinctly uneasy. "I need a reason to socialize with the Island's residents. I won't be telling you anything that isn't common knowledge when I admit we don't have much in the way of leads. The slickness of our thief indicates that he has an inside source of information. He only hits when the owners are gone from home. Apparently he has access to the security keys that operate the alarm. How, we still haven't discovered. He takes only those items that are easily portable, and he comes and goes without anyone seeing one blessed thing."

"Maybe he is just especially lucky." He didn't believe it even as he said it.

Lacy gave him a look that said more than words. "Three times in a row? It would be different if he was hitting the houses that have already closed up for the season, but he isn't. So far, he is staying with the homes where the owners are attending various social functions. On the surface that doesn't make a lot of sense."

"It would if he was establishing an alibi," he commented, drawn in to speculating on the unknown culprit.

Lacy blinked in surprise at his deduction. David caught her expression and grinned.

"I may be an architect, but that doesn't mean I can't think."

"I never implied you were stupid," she returned, disturbed that she had given him that impression. "Some people just aren't tuned to puzzles."

"Remind me to invite you over Sunday for a session over the New York Times crossword puzzle."

Lacy groaned. "Don't tell me you're one of those that can do the thing in minutes."

He smiled, not denying the charge. "Get back to work, woman. We both need some sleep sometime tonight."

"There isn't really much more. I can't hide that I am a detective, but I thought I'd toss a little smoke about. If we are seen to date, it not only gives me a reason to be on the Island in more than a professional capacity but it will also, I hope, lull our man into believing that I'm too distracted by your manly charms to be much of a threat."

David grimaced at the description. "I wish you would have put that another way."

"Got your ego, did I?"

She couldn't resist teasing him. The comfort of her position, the feel of him against her side had all but dispelled her headache, leaving behind a relaxation that was growing by the second. She was enjoying herself, she realized. She shouldn't be, for certainly the situation was serious. Yet, she couldn't deny that sharing her work with David was more than pleasant. Only with John had she approached this kind of communication. She studied David without seeming to. The sight of his long body stretched in a pose similar to her own brought to mind the feel of his body against hers when he had kissed her.

"What are you thinking?" David leaned toward her, his gaze searching her half-closed eyes. She had the look of a contented kitten just before it dropped off to sleep. The drowsy expression called up tender feelings he didn't know he possessed. With any other woman he would have been considering how to get her in bed and himself wrapped around sexy female curves. But not with Lacy, or at least, not unless she was going to sleep, preferably with him beside her.

"Nothing," Lacy whispered untruthfully.

He smiled, knowing she lied. "We're going out tonight." It was both a statement and a question.

"Yes."

"That's just what I like. No argument." He stroked her neck, his fingers slipping caressingly over the delicate length.

Lacy hardly noticed his words. The pleasure of his touch held more importance. She tipped her head to give him better access to her body. His light stroking sent shivers through her, pleasuring without demanding anything of her. "Where will we go?" No matter how much she tried to remember she shouldn't be allowing him to touch her this way, she still found she could not deny either of them.

"Dinner," David replied absently, absorbed in watching her lashes dust over her cheeks as she relaxed more fully into the cushions cradling her.

"What time?" Lacy asked the questions out of reflex more than curiosity. She felt as if she were drifting on a warm cloud, free, untouched by the concerns and worries of reality. The feeling was as new to her as the man who called it forth from the depths of her weary body.

"Seven, all right?"

"Mmmm."

David smiled at the long drawn-out sound. It was as close as he had ever heard a human come to a purr. "You should be in bed."

"So should you."

He chuckled softly. "Believe me, the thought had crossed my mind. I don't suppose we could sleep together if I promise to stay on my side of the mattress?"

"Could you keep a promise like that?" Lacy wanted to know without opening her eyes.

"No."

"Then two people, two beds." The effort it took to lift her lashes was more than she wanted to exert. Only the need to see his face made her try. The lack of disappointment in his expression came as a mild surprise. The man had just made a pass, and he didn't appear in the least upset that she had turned him down. In fact, he looked as though her answer was exactly what he had expected.

"You're a nice person," she murmured, watching him.

He wasn't a nice person. He was a fool because he cared enough to not take advantage of her when she was too tired to fight him. "Damned with faint praise," David replied, gazing at her as closely as she did him. "If you weren't looking like you needed a week of rest and if I wasn't so bushed myself, I'd show you just how nice I can be."

She smiled, a slow, sleepy kind of smile that gave David ideas that he could have well done without.

"And unless you want me to change my mind, stop that," he added, removing his hand from the tempting curve of her throat. It would be so easy to slip it around the nape of her neck and draw her to his chest. Her lips were parted as though waiting for his kiss.

"Stop what?" Her brows lifted in a leisurely challenge.

David groaned. There was just so much one man could take when a woman flexed her femininity in his direction. Before sanity prevailed, he bent his head to taste of her just one more time. Her lips opened to him. His tongue slid with agonizing slowness into her mouth, stroking, pleasuring with each thrust. His hands pulled her to him, molding her to his body where she belonged. He felt the tremor that rippled through her and tore at the rigid control that kept him from taking more than this one taste. For long moments, he feasted on her mouth, learning the texture and shape with erotic thoroughness.

Lacy sighed, feeling the warmth of his body seep into her marrow, revitalizing her limbs. Her fingers slipped through his hair, enjoying the silken strands and sounds of pleasure he made at her touch. Part of her knew it was madness to indulge herself this way, yet she was in no mood to play it safe. She wanted him. It was that simple. Whether today or next week, it made little difference.

"Have you changed your mind?" David asked huskily, lifting his head enough to search her expression. She felt so good in his arms. He tightened his hold, imprinting himself on her body. He wanted the memory of this moment to be stronger than the wariness that shielded her from him.

Lacy lay in his arms, looking up at him. He could take her now and they both knew it. She hadn't meant to give in to him and they both knew that as well. Part of her wanted him to take the decision from her hands. For the first time in her life she didn't want to be self-sufficient.

"I want to," she admitted, unable to lie.

"But you won't." He fought back the temptation to change her mind.

"I can't."

Both noted the difference in wording. "And after?"

Lacy smiled faintly. "Now who's asking questions that only the devil himself has the answers to?"

Using the tip of his forefinger, David traced the outline of her lips. "I'm going to change your mind," he warned. David lifted his finger to kiss her quickly, hard. "So be prepared," he whispered before getting to his feet. He stopped her when she would have gotten up. "No, stay there. I'll let myself out."

Before Lacy could move, he was gone. Minutes slipped by as she stared at the doorway through which he had passed. No thoughts filled her mind. No questions teased the bump of curiosity that had been her virtue and curse since she was born. She quite simply was warm, relaxed and content. She neither knew what lay between her and David—now or in the future. For the first time in her life she would go forth without knowing what lay around the next corner.

Six
_____

Lacy slid out of her car, leaving the window down against the unseasonable warmth of the noon sun. There was nothing she hated more than getting into a stifling hot car. Glancing around, she sized up the house of Sarah and Samuel Mann. So far, this morning had been a total bust. First, the fingerprints lifted from the Dellwoods' had turned out to be only those of the two sisters. Then Garrick had called the office practically frothing at the mouth over the latest burglary. John hadn't been in a much better frame of mind when she had explained about enlisting David's help. Then she had made the call to Sarah Mann, explaining that she was a co-worker of her husband's. She had felt like a betrayer when, on learning Lacy was going to be in the neighborhood, Sarah had extended an invitation to visit. All things considered, Lacy was beginning to wish she had stayed in bed and caught up on her sleep.

She sighed, knowing she couldn't put this interview off any longer, and started up the walk. A slight breeze stirred, barely touching her skin with the promise of the winter that showed on the calender but not in the weather. She rang the doorbell and waited. Nothing happened. Moments passed and still no one came to open the door. No sounds came from the interior.

She tried again. Finally she heard the slow steps coming nearer. Then the door swung open. Lacy blessed the training that kept the smile of greeting on her face. The sight of the tiny creature before her made her want to cry in sympathy, until she looked into Sarah Mann's eyes.

While her illness had long since destroyed any looks she had ever had, her eyes held peace and a kind of contentment with life that was as unexpected as it was beautiful. If Sam loved his wife, and Lacy had known that day by the tone of his voice that he did, then was it not possible that he would risk anything to give this woman happiness? Lacy extended her hand and introduced herself. What she was about to do made her uncomfortable, but she had no choice. She hated subterfuge, and she hated more the thought of hurting an innocent.

"I'm so glad you invited me over. Sam speaks so much of you." Lacy uttered the lies, wishing she could tell the truth. "He said you didn't get out much," she explained gently, weaving a tapestry of fiction and fact.

The gaunt face creased into a smile of welcome as Sarah stepped back to allow Lacy to enter. "It was sweet of you to think of me...." Her voice trailed off. Then she smiled brightly.

Lacy forced her emotions into the far corner of her mind. If she didn't, she wouldn't be able to go through with her questions. Everything about Sarah made her wish there was another way. "What a lovely home you have,'' Lacy murmured, following her hostess through the living room.

Sarah led the way to a cosily furnished, glass-enclosed patio off the compact kitchen. Everywhere Lacy turned she found possessions to delight the eye. Tiny boxes decorated with dainty cameo faces atop delicate occasional tables, colorful glass figures against an open window and fresh-cut flowers from the lush bounty of the backyard garden were scattered about the house. Sam's love and thoughtfulness for his dying wife were evident in each touch.

Sarah waved Lacy to a chair. "May I make you a cup of tea?"

"Only if you allow me to help. I've been sitting all morning and would welcome a change."

Lacy moved to take the kettle from the frail fingers. The look Sarah gave her held understanding although she didn't voice it. Instead, she turned to a cabinet and pulled out an assortment of teas and a box of fancy chocolates. Lacy noted the presence of the expensive candy with a feeling of dismay. After seeing Sarah she didn't want Sam to be involved with the thefts. The sweets weren't evidence that any court would recognize, but Lacy couldn't ignore what having the costly but frivolous candy might mean. With Sam's bills, it was impossible he had the money to afford such gifts unless there was an outside source of income. The knickknacks that added such charm to Sarah's life didn't come cheap. Some might have been around before her illness, but most looked too new. So how was Sam affording this life-style? That's what Lacy had to find out if she could.

"Are you a chocolate fancier?" Lacy asked as she filled the china teapot with hot water.

Sarah grinned, suddenly displaying a glimpse of the beauty she must have had in her youth. "Guilty." She waved a hand around the room. "I'm very spoiled as you can see. Sam indulges me shamelessly. We had a two-story house for a long time, you know. But those stairs. And there wasn't such a large yard for my flowers either. So Sam bought this little place for me. I just love it." She placed the chocolates on the table and then lifted the cake dome to pull out a crystal plate arranged with tiny decorated tea cakes.

Lacy was no stranger to those. They came from a bakery in Palm Beach, and they cost more than she wanted to remember, having bought some for a small dinner party she had given last year. One more clue to point in Sam's direction. Yet there could be another explanation, too. Perhaps the move from the larger house to the smaller one had provided the unexplained income.

"I just wish he wouldn't work so hard. He's so rarely home anymore. I don't really need all these little things." A gentle sigh punctuated her regret.

"Work so hard? Is he working extra hours? I didn't realize," she murmured, probing carefully. According to the time cards, Mann hadn't put in any overtime in months.

"I really couldn't say," Sarah replied vaguely. "He doesn't have much time to spend in the garden anymore. My flowers are suffering so." She stared out the window, her face creased with lines of worry.

Lacy settled down to a light, entertaining visit to brighten Sarah's hours and at the same time accomplish her mission. It was after two before she took her leave. The time hadn't been a complete loss, but it also hadn't provided many answers—just more questions.

One thing had emerged of note, and that was a reference to a man named Willy that Sarah didn't like. No amount of probing had produced any more information beyond the fact that Sam had some sort of business arrangement with the man. Armed with her findings, Lacy decided to tackle Sam. She had never told Sarah who she really was, but she had no doubt Sam would put two and two together as soon as he heard about her visit. She couldn't afford to allow him to get over the jolt of her tactics. She wanted to use that shock to its best advantage if she could. So instead of letting Sarah break the news, she would do it herself and be on hand to observe Sam's reactions.

It took an hour to catch the accountant in his office, alone. Finally, she confronted him with only the width of a desk between them. Without seeming to, she studied him carefully. Outwardly, he appeared relaxed but his hands gave him away. They twisted the pencil he held nervously.

"I saw your wife today," she said bluntly. If Sam was involved she wanted to know now before the thefts got any worse, or someone got hurt. With only three jobs to his credit and the clear desperation of his case, he just might have a chance with a sympathetic jury.

"You what?" he demanded, staring at her. "You had no right." Anger and fear tightened his voice, adding depth to the normally gentle tones.

Lacy held her reactions at bay. She had to seem tough, hard. She had to get the answers she needed, not just for the case, but for him as well. "We had a long talk."

"If you have upset her in any way," he ground out, surging to his feet and planting clenched fists on the desk.

Lacy eyed his belligerent stance, then his face. "You'll what?" His reaction wasn't answering one question be-

yond the depth of his love for his wife. And if he was innocent, she was pushing him hard, hurting him through
the love he had for Sarah. If he was guilty, maybe she
could help him out of the mess he had made. Either way
she had to live with what she was doing.

"You know why I was hired. You also know everyone
connected with Garrick's is suspect. I've got a copy of
your credit report and it reads like a nightmare. I have
seen your wife, your home and those luxuries that you
surround her with. That takes money. You don't have
any. So you tell me what you're up to. Where the cash is
coming from. Who's Willy? What are you doing late at
night and on the weekends? And before you refuse,
think. So far, no one has been hurt. Whoever our man is,
he's not always going to be as lucky as he's been so far.
Then what? The crime stops being a few treasures pur-
loined. It becomes assault and all the rest and that's provided the victim doesn't die. What happens to Sarah
then? Who'll take care of her if you aren't there to do
it?"

"I don't know what you are talking about, I tell you,"
Sam shouted, beside himself with fear and worry. "Yes,
I bought Sarah things but not with stolen money. I earned
every penny. You can check. I can prove it." He jerked
away from the desk and took his briefcase from the shelf
behind him. Fumbling at the locks, he opened it and extracted a folder crammed with papers. "I've been
moonlighting. That's against company policy. Garrick
would fire me if he knew, and I must have both these
jobs. You saw Sarah." His eyes pleaded with her, his
voice begged her to believe him.

This was the part of her job Lacy hated, really hated.
She didn't need to open the folder to know Sam spoke the

truth, but she did anyway. Despite her belief she still had to check his story out. She said as much.

"Of course. Just don't bother Sarah again, please."

"She has no idea who I am or why I came to see her." That at least she could give this poor man and gladly. "She simply thinks I am a temporary co-worker who happened to be in the neighborhood and stopped by for tea and a chat. Unless you tell her, she'll never know any differently." Lacy tapped the folder. "That's assuming this checks out." No threat was intended. It was the simple truth.

Sam sagged in his seat, realizing that she had been kinder than he thought. "How could you have questioned her without telling her who you were?" he asked, puzzled. "Why would you protect either of us?"

Lacy stood. She had accomplished what she'd set out to do. "I didn't protect you or anyone. I just didn't jump to conclusions without some facts to back myself up." In her business she couldn't afford being thought soft. Her professional image was sometimes the difference between success and failure.

Sam looked at her, clearly trying to work out her meaning. "But how did you get Sarah to tell you all that stuff about Willy and my moonlighting?"

"Your wife is a very trusting and very special lady." She smiled as she spoke, for one moment a woman and not a detective. "She likes talking about you."

Sam's face reddened slightly. "Thank you," he mumbled.

Lacy's brows raised at the expression of gratitude. "For what?"

"For not hurting her when it would have made your job easier."

His gratitude made her feel like a fraud. "You're very forgiving after what you just went through."

He shook his head. "Realistic. I've had to be the last few years." The resignation in his words was no bid for sympathy but simply a statement of fact.

Lacy did both of them the honor of accepting it as such. "If this checks out, this afternoon never happened."

He inclined his head. There was nothing more either of them could say.

Lacy left Garrick's knowing that she had just eliminated another suspect. The process had left a dirty taste in her mouth despite Sam's understanding. She wanted nothing more than a hot bath and some time alone. She got neither. The moment she was in the car there was a call on the car phone. It was one of her informers demanding a meet. The time was set for an hour. Since it was almost five that would mean she'd really be cutting it close to make her date with David. For a second she debated calling him, then decided against it. If she was late it would only be by a few minutes.

She couldn't have been more wrong. The informer arrived after her. Then she discovered that he was only a go-between. It took another thirty minutes to get to the real source of the information, a shadowy form in a car on a deserted stretch of road, west of Jupiter. Lacy got out of her car and approached the other vehicle, alert to the possible dangers of the situation. A window slid down a few inches, then a raspy voice spoke.

"Ain't pro. Only one man. On the Island." Then the car with the blackened license drove away leaving Lacy staring after it.

Lacy was past being surprised by anything. She got in her car and left the area, her mind already sifting through

the short words. Not enough. Too much. The tip was
both. She had recognized the source of the information
and knew the tip was no phony trail. She could believe
what she'd been told. The field was slowly narrowing. If
their thief wasn't a pro, he would make a mistake eventually that would provide a real lead. And if that part
about being on the Island meant he lived there, then she
was all the more glad David had agreed to help her.

David! She'd forgotten all about him. A quick glance
at her watch showed it was past eight. She groaned
deeply. What must he be thinking? She found out in short
order. David was sitting in his car waiting for her when
she got home.

"Where have you been?" he demanded, glaring at her.
He'd been imagining all sorts of trouble.

Lacy sighed, knowing his anger was justified. "I had
to meet one of my street people, but he was late."

David stared at her as though she had taken leave of
her senses. It took a moment for him to understand the
slang, and when he did he was anything but appeased.
"Street people? As in bums, derelicts and druggies?" he
asked with a dangerous calm.

Lacy eyed his hostile face, suddenly realizing that more
than her tardy arrival was driving him. "Sometimes," she
replied slowly. The fear that flashed across his face was
as unmistakable as it was surprising.

"Alone?" He swallowed on the question, knowing the
answer, whether she gave it to him or not.

"Yes." Lacy didn't understand. She was so accustomed to the risks of her profession that she only noticed the ones she had to actively deal with.

"And your uncle allows you to do this?" When he
thought of her job he had thought of the fact-finding as-

pect of it. The danger hadn't been very real. Now it was, in spades.

"Of course. It's part of the job."

David tried to be calm, but the thought of what could happen to a beautiful woman such as Lacy in the rough world she walked in and out of every day scared him out of his normal poise. And the horror of it was, she seemed completely unaware of the danger. Even now she watched him with the puzzled look that said she had a dozen questions buzzing in her head. The need to hold her was stronger than his willpower. He pulled her into his arms and buried his face against her neck.

"You're crazy. Do you know that?"

Lacy yielded to her own needs. It had been a long day, filled with things she would rather not remember. In his arms she could forget, if only for a little while. "No, I don't know that," she whispered.

"Believe me, you are. You could have been hurt and you don't even realize it."

Now she understood the fear. It was for her. The warmth of the caring that would prompt him to worry about her went through her with unexpected strength. No one, that she could remember, had ever been afraid for her. Not even John, her closest relative. He knew the risks, accepting them, and had taught her how to do the same.

"It wasn't that dangerous," she tried to console him. "In fact, our work rarely is. Most of it is very boring if you want to know the truth. The only danger one of us is really in, is getting sick from eating too many take-away meals while we're either following an erring husband or watching a cheating wife."

He didn't believe her, but he could sense she wanted him to. So he pretended, folding her against his chest.

"How long will it take you to dress? Or would you rather eat in?" If he didn't keep his mind on mundane things he would carry her into her house and teach her in the most primitive way possible just how much she was coming to mean to him. He cared, even if no one else in her crazy world worried about her.

One more defense crumbled with his words. No man had ever seen that she needed peace, not a crowded restaurant after a grueling day. She wanted to simply unwind, munch on whatever came to hand and curl up in her oldest clothes. But she had promised him a dinner date, and she always kept her word. "Just give me a minute."

David frowned, looking at her. "Don't do that," he said almost angrily.

Lacy lifted her head, not understanding his tone or the words. "Do what?"

"Pretend. I hate it when you do."

"I don't pretend."

"Don't you? Right now you don't want to go anywhere. Don't you think I know that? But you're going. Why? Why can't you just say you need to relax? Would it be so terrible to admit you aren't a superwoman?"

Hurt slipped in before Lacy could guard against the intrusion. "Is that what you think I'm doing? Trying to be superwoman?"

David opened his mouth to say yes, then thought better of it. The light caught Lacy's eyes, showing him pain and a kind of weariness that was outside his experience. She looked...vulnerable. Young, but so very old in ways he could only guess at. Suddenly he saw how very far apart their lives were. He had never known real danger, never seen a violent death and wouldn't know where to begin to do the job she did every day.

Unsure of himself and her, he sought refuge in a half answer. "I think you are so accustomed to being independent that you forget you don't need to be that self-sufficient at every moment of your life," he replied finally.

Lacy could accept that. "Perhaps," she agreed, relaxing against him once more.

David eased her away from his chest. "Now go take a shower and change while I order us something to eat."

Lacy smiled at his take-charge tone. "All right, but I'm only doing this because I'm too hungry to wait to get dressed, us to drive—"

David silenced her with a swift kiss. "Be quiet, woman, and just go. I get the message."

Lacy went, almost. Halfway up the stairs she remembered what she was still wearing. Reaching under her jacket she pulled out the small automatic tucked in the special holster in the middle of her lower back. The weapon fit smoothly into the contour of her spine, offering a concealment that no shoulder holster had ever given her. Turning, gun in hand, she retraced her steps without thinking. David's sharp indrawn breath stopped her before she reached the bottom stair. She froze. His eyes were riveted on the gun as though he had never seen one before.

"How long have you been wearing that?" he asked hoarsely. "Every time we have gone out?"

"No, of course not. There was no need." Lacy came down the rest of the way, stopping only when she stood before him. "Does it bother you that much?" she said, watching him closely. Shock was in his expression, and a kind of horror, too. The first was understandable, the second, worrying.

"But you do wear this thing when you work?" he persisted, wondering how he had missed the possibility that she was armed. Common sense should have told him she would be.

"Not always. Only when it's necessary. Like tonight." She wanted him to understand, Lacy realized as she faced him. More than anyone she had ever known she wanted David to accept what she did and the things she had to do to protect herself. If he could not... Her mind halted on that point. If he could not, what? He was neither lover nor husband. Their relationship was too new for either of them to make demands on the other.

David studied the slim hand holding the automatic with such ease. She knew how to use the thing. May have even used it on another human. He wouldn't ask.

"You said yourself how dangerous it was to meet that man tonight," Lacy pointed out. "Would you rather I went into a potentially dangerous situation without any protection?" He was so quiet, withdrawn. Lacy felt the wall between them and the hurt his withdrawal was creating within her. She didn't want him to see her the way others saw her. She wanted him to understand.

David inhaled slowly, striving for control. There was more at stake here than just the gun. It was his way of life against hers. All of his life he had known where he was going and how he would get there. Until Lacy. Nothing about her was familiar or comprehensible. Yet he tried to bridge the differences between them. He wanted to know her, how she thought, who she was. To do that he had to accept her work.

"No, of course not. I just didn't think," he explained, watching her as closely as she watched him. The bewilderment, the plea for understanding, was so clear that it hurt him to look at her.

"I never wear it unless I have to," she whispered, trying to appease him without realizing it.

David lifted his fingers to touch the soft curve of her cheek. "It was the surprise of seeing it, that's all," he murmured, wanting to see the worry leave her eyes, more than he needed to sort out his own feelings. There would be time enough for that later.

Lacy searched his face, almost afraid to believe he wasn't pulling away. Every man before him had. She looked into his eyes, trying to read answers in their silvery blue depths. All she found was sincerity and tenderness.

"Let me just put this in my handbag, then I'll shower and change."

David pulled back his hand, turning away. "I'll go make that call."

"The number for the best pizza place in town is on the refrigerator. They even deliver," Lacy called, stifling the urge to follow him to the kitchen.

Both of them needed a moment alone. For a second she silently cursed the informer who had brought her to this confrontation. If she hadn't been so rushed for time she would have remembered to take the gun off and put it away before she had gotten home. Then David wouldn't have bumped rock hard against her work. With no preparation, seeing a gun in her hand was bound to be a shock. But he had tried to understand, which was more than most of the men in her past had ever done. David had cared enough to listen.

She hugged the truth to herself, feeling vulnerable in a way she had never known. All her defenses, all her past experiences were no longer of any use. David was slowly slipping through her guard to her soul. With others she would have fought the intrusion; with David all she wanted to do was surrender. She stared at herself in the mirror, seeing a softness that was new on her own face. It was like looking at the birth of a new woman, kind of scary but exciting, too. She looked at her body with new eyes, liking the physical beauty of her form. She wanted to please him. She wanted him to find her face and figure desirable, feminine, sexy. She wanted to tempt that control of his until he took her because he could not help himself.

Seven

"Where do you suppose she keeps the glasses?" David muttered under his breath.

So far he had opened three cabinets and unearthed two boxes of Oreos, seven containers of laundry detergent, Christmas bows, cocktail napkins and a can of coffee. What he hadn't seen was any order, any organization to a room that should have demanded it. What didn't pertain to her job, Lacy seemed to ignore. The more he learned of her the more he realized how complete her dedication to her craft had been in the past. Yet he could sense changes now. He had touched her and he wanted to reach her even more, to show her the world she seemed to have forgotten or tucked away somewhere as though it did not exist. As he finished readying the table for their meal, he wondered what had caused her to bury herself so deeply in her career. It was almost as if she were hiding or protecting something. He frowned as the thought entered his mind and refused to leave. He had seen the softness in her, the vulnerability. Could what she did hurt her so much that she had to become this controlled woman he had seen far too often for his liking? The idea hurt him in ways he barely understood. If he was right, Lacy was only half-alive, buried under the demands she had forced on herself.

Lacy came into the room just as he finished. "You have no idea how nice this is," she said, meaning every word. She missed his frown completely.

David glanced up, startled at the heartfelt tone. "What?"

Lacy waved her hand to encompass his preparations. "I detest eating alone. And I especially hate having to fix everything just for one."

"You call this fixing?"

He stared at the less than fancy arrangement he had produced. No flowers. No candles. Nothing unusual about anything he had done. Yet he could tell Lacy was being honest in her response. Puzzled, curious, he stared at her. For every question she answered, three popped up to tantalize him.

The doorbell rang, signaling the arrival of the pizzas. Lacy took the money David offered her, went to answer it, leaving him to open the wine. She returned carrying two cardboard boxes that looked too huge for just the two of them.

"You ordered enough to feed an army," Lacy said with a laugh as she returned to the kitchen. She opened the first container, sniffing appreciatively.

"I wasn't sure how hungry you were. Besides, I happen to like pizza. When I was in college I practically lived on the stuff. The cheesier the better." He joined her, standing just behind her. Leaning over her shoulder to survey the spread gave him an excellent excuse to touch her.

Lacy turned her head, her lips just inches from his. She forgot about the rendezvous in the darkness, the gun she carried, the case, everything but the man who touched her with controlled strength and teased her with laughter in his eyes and on his lips. "All those long years ago."

"It seems like another lifetime." He grinned at her. Her lips looked ready to kiss. He made them both wait. He wouldn't rush, for he wanted more. "I'm a respectable businessman now who spends more time in sit-down restaurants these days." Her body curved into his. Her softness against his toughness. He lifted his hands to her shoulders, easing her around until she faced him. "You're so very beautiful."

Lacy gazed at him, not expecting the compliment. She had wanted him to notice that she had put on a soft lounging gown that flowed over her body like a silk drape. She had wanted him to see the turquoise color made her eyes more green than brown. But more than that she had wanted him to take her in his arms and hold her again.

"Thank you."

He smiled. Even in accepting a compliment she was different from most women. No coyness, no surprise, just truth spoken out of need. Slipping his hands up her shoulders he brought her closer yet. "I'm going to kiss you."

"I wish you would." She raised her head slightly. She had never been so forthright with a man, never felt free enough to be vulnerable.

David gazed into her eyes as he bent his head. "Look at me," he commanded when she would have shut her eyes.

Lacy watched, mesmerized, as his lips came down on hers. Lightly, teasingly, he traced the contours of her mouth with his tongue. She tried to capture the moist tip, but he evaded her.

"Please," she whispered. "Don't tease."

"Never that. Only pleasure," he murmured before taking what she was so eager to give.

Lacy sighed deeply as he filled her senses with his taste and feel. His hands held her as though he was protecting and possessing at the same time. She couldn't move closer or farther away. All she could do was feel. She ran her hands through his hair as she groaned against his mouth. Desire rippled through her, heightening her perceptions, closing down her world until it contained only the two of them.

David ended the kiss at the last moment of his control. One more second and he wouldn't have cared that she was tired, that he wanted to give her pampering and tenderness as well as passion. "I think the pizza's getting cold," he whispered, pressing one last kiss to her lips.

Lacy laughed unsteadily. "Then it's the only thing in the room that is." She sank into the chair he pulled out for her. Her legs felt as though they had the consistency of bread dough. Even her hands were shaking.

David took a chair next to her. "Honey, I like your style," he said, lifting her fingers to his lips.

There are an infinite variety of places in a relationship to discover that there is more to your wanting a man than just passion. Lacy found her spot in that moment. She looked in David's eyes, saw the laughter, the tenderness and the desire there and knew that he would be her lover. Not because she couldn't say no. Not because she had caught him. But because he had made a place in her life for himself. He hadn't forced, he hadn't taken. He had quite simply slipped under her guard and overwhelmed her defenses. He saw things about her that no one else did. He took care of her when she would have allowed no one to even know she needed someone. But most of all he made her like herself again and not feel as if she had to be tougher than she really was.

"And I like yours."

The pizzas were no longer hot, but neither of them really noticed. Conversation ebbed and flowed without touching on anything of real importance. When they finished and were lingering over the last of the wine David had unearthed, he said, "I just remembered. You know everything there is to know about me. How about returning the favor." There was no rancor in his voice. He had accepted her need to investigate him and had put the issue aside.

Lacy sipped from her glass, considering her answer. "Let's see. I was born of average, very loving parents. My early years were quite ordinary. I had all the childhood diseases at the right time, dated when all the other girls started and managed to graduate without disgracing myself or John with horrible grades. By then my family had been killed in a car accident." For a second she remembered that dark time. Then the sweetness of the years that followed lessened the old pain.

"When John came into my life he was a bachelor and totally unsuited—his words not mine—to caring for a teenage female. The only experience he had with my sex was the type he was damn sure he didn't want me to know about or experience. They say there is nothing worse than a reformed rake for guarding a woman's virtue. Whoever wrote that knew John. Anyway, we both survived, although not without a claw mark or two. His temper is nearly as explosive as mine." She frowned a bit, considering the last part. "On second thought, I think it's very possibly worse."

"What made you decide to join him in the agency?"

"A fluke, actually." Lacy grinned, remembering how she had become a part of the team. "All through high school, I couldn't settle on one career that truly appealed. John tried to help, the school counselors tried as well and so did I. Nothing called me. The summer after I graduated, John's secretary came down with mono, a terrible case. He tried a few temps, but by the time they had dealt with his temper for more than a day they gave notice. I offered to help out since I had taken typing in school. He was right in the middle of a big insurance-fraud case at the time."

"I can guess what's coming," David inserted, watching her changing expressions intently.

Lacy chuckled, her eyes dancing with mischief at his tone. "It had more twists than a crooked road. I couldn't resist trying to figure out who was cheating who. Or is it whom?" She tilted her head to one side.

David waved a hand in a dismissive gesture. "I can't remember, nor do I care. Get on with it."

"Impatient male," she murmured, collecting her thoughts to finish her story.

His glare was halfhearted at best.

"Anyway..." She stopped to sip her wine. David sighed. She lifted her eyes, grinning at his expression.

"If you aren't murdered before this night's over it won't be because I haven't thought about it," he warned, enjoying her playful mood. He wondered if she realized how beautiful she looked with the soft light dancing in her hair and the glow of amusement sparkling in her eyes.

Lacy ignored the threat. "It turned out the brother of the senior partner was responsible for the scam. He'd been living with his relative for years and knew all the details of the business and what to do to pull off the fraud.''

''I don't see how that stood to help him out unless his brother was an accomplice.'' The words didn't matter. Watching her did.

''Believe me, none of us could figure it out at first either. The older man was ill and had intended to sell out to the younger even though he had not been interested in the business. Family feeling, that sort of thing. The younger knew his limitations and had decided to unload his heritage as soon as possible. But he loved his sibling enough to worry what that kind of move would do to their relationship. So he devised a plan to burn down the main part of the building, including the lion's share of the stock. His brother was too ill to bother with reconstruction and the damaged property would fetch a lower price. He bought it, then sold it to a syndicate after pocketing the insurance money.''

David stared at her, finally paying attention to the story. ''And you figured this out?''

She inclined her head, enjoying his look of shock. ''Your expression reminds me of John's when I laid the scenario out for him,'' she said, laughing a little.

''The mind boggles.''

''John was a bit more eloquent.''

''He's had more experience with the way your brain works,'' he replied, torn between admiration for her deductive powers and disbelief over the case that had brought them to light.

''That's true.'' She poured herself another glass of wine. Now that she had eaten her fill, she felt the tension and exhaustion seep from her body. David was there, smiling at her, touching her. It was enough for now.

Leaning back in her chair, she allowed her eyes to drift half-closed.

David heard the soft sigh that slipped from her lips. A tiny frown worked into his brow. Even the muted light didn't completely hide the shadows beneath Lacy's eyes. The tension that had drawn her so tight was gone at last. A wave of pleasure filled him to know that he was responsible for the relief she was experiencing.

"Why don't you curl up on the couch in the living room while I clean up this mess," he suggested quietly.

"I can't leave you to do this," Lacy protested halfheartedly.

"You can and you will." David rose in one smooth motion and came around to her side of the table. Before Lacy could protest he lifted her in his arms, pausing only long enough to look down at her. "Just be quiet and let me do for you tonight. You can repay me the next time I come in so wiped out that I wouldn't make a good dust cloth."

Lacy laughed. She seemed to be doing a lot of that around this man. "Fair enough," she agreed, looping her arms around his neck and tucking her head under his chin. "Just don't expect me to carry you about."

He smiled at the tacked-on condition. "You have my word of honor," he said as solemnly as a judge, stifling the urge to do more than just hold her.

The need to sink into the cushions and drink his fill of her lips was strong. But the need to cherish her was more potent. Cherish was such an old-fashioned word for a very modern woman. Yet it was exactly how he felt, he realized as he laid her on the couch. For a moment he leaned over her, searching her drowsy eyes. There was a flicker of desire in the green depths, buried beneath the exhaustion that shadowed her face. The temptation to fan the small ember was there, growing with each second he spent poised above her body. Yet he could not make himself move. Not yet.

"I want·you," Lacy whispered, raising her hand to touch his cheek. "I've never had the nerve to say that out loud to any man until now."

David closed his eyes for an instant, surprised and more pleased than he should have been at the admission. "Are you sure?" he asked before opening his lashes to watch her with more hunger than he knew.

"Very." She slipped her arms around his shoulders, intending to draw him down to her. His resistance came as a shock. Suddenly she realized he was no longer looking at her but at something behind her head. She turned, at first not seeing anything unusual. Then her eyes focused on her handbag. The gun. If he had shouted the words she wouldn't have been any more aware of the problem than she was at that moment. His withdrawal was so subtle she would have missed it if she had not been touching him.

"Not tonight. You need your rest."

David caught her hands and drew them from his body. For a second his mind warred with his physical needs. His fingers tightened. One glance told him Lacy had seen far more than he wanted her to. The knowledge of the barrier between them lay in her eyes, though she said nothing. She let him fold her hands across her stomach. She even allowed the light touch he trailed down her cheek.

"I'm going to clean up the dining room and then let myself out." He winced at the way his words sounded.

"And tomorrow? We had a date to go sailing." Lacy stared at him, wondering if he had any idea what his attitude was doing to her.

"It's still on. I'll pick you up at eight." He straightened, hating the way he was acting but powerless to change. Seeing that handbag, knowing what was inside, had brought the danger of the life she led back to him. For a moment he had been able to forget, had wanted to forget.

"Wear something warm tomorrow. It will be cold out on the water," he murmured, speaking without really hearing what he was saying.

The command, coupled with the concern in his voice, said so much more than the way he stepped away from her. Lacy watched him as he walked to the door without looking back. She could have called him to her side. He might even have come. But she held her tongue. The demon riding him was one she had lost to before. David would either defeat the specter of her work, or he would go the way of those in her past. Loneliness stared her in the face yet again. This time the feeling was intensified beyond anything she had known. In a few short days David had shown her a glimpse of a world she had yet to experience. He had made her laugh when she had wanted to curse in frustration. He had cared enough to comfort her, to worry about her in a way no one had done. But more than that he had made her suspect that her life was missing some important ingredient, an ingredient he knew about and she had yet to discover.

The faint sounds of dishes penetrated the quiet of the town house. Even now, when every instinct in him was probably telling him to leave, to put some distance between them, David was there caring for her.

Why?

The question slipped into her mind to become a demand that she couldn't dislodge. For the first time ever she tried to push the small word far away, out of reach.

She was afraid to question because she was afraid of the answers.

Lacy heard the door close on David as he left. A sigh rose from the depths of her being as she got up from the couch. She had been a fool. She had no one else to blame but herself for her career and the demands that even now she knowingly accepted. Wrapping her arms around her stomach, she tried to warm the sudden chill that passed over her skin. It was hard, this path she had chosen. To walk alone was something she had been doing for a long time, something that should have been second nature for the woman she had become.

"Stupid! Fool!" David's muttered comments punctuated his footsteps as he left Lacy's place. He got in the car and slammed the door, something he never did. Lead foot he wasn't, although no one but he would have known that a half hour later. The circling blue light on the highway patrol's car cast an intermittent glow over the interior of his vehicle. As he reached in his back pocket for his driver's license and registration, David silently added a few choice oaths to the now-constant refrain of fool and stupid.

Minutes later he tossed the signed speeding ticket on the seat beside him. A week ago he would have thought anyone getting a citation needed his head examined. With the limit signs posted everywhere there was no excuse for disobeying the rules. The realization of how regimented, staid was a better word, he had become was inescapable. Witness him being upset, even unnerved, by the fact that Lacy carried a gun for protection in a potentially hazardous situation. Here was an intriguing, challenging woman, and he was expecting her to be an average female with ordinary interests. When he found out she wasn't, what did he do? He got angry. How dare she not

tell him who and what she was. He was David Marsh III
of the David Marshes of Maryland. She needed his as-
sistance. She asked him. Did he help? Oh, no. He was no
spy. Even now the memory of that unfair accusation
haunted him. Then his godmother got robbed. David
Marsh to the rescue. He would make the thief pay for
daring to pick on one of his family.

"Arrogant fool." He spit the words out.

If he had been Lacy he would have refused the offer as
well. And then came the biggest folly of all. While he
wasn't an avid hunter he did know how to handle fire-
arms. Did he remember that? Not him. He acted like a
first-class jerk who not only had never seen a gun before
but was totally against its use on the planet earth. It was
a wonder that Lacy hadn't brained him with the nearest
blunt object. And let's not forget the stupidity of the man
who left rather than talk out his feelings. Was Lacy so
unapproachable? Far from it. The woman had class and
an honesty he admired. What did he have? A lame excuse a first-grader could have seen through.

David pulled into the garage and got out, without
really noticing that he had arrived home. "I blew it."

"Sir?" The butler opened the door.

David ignored the diffident query to continue on his
way to the study. "That will be all for tonight," he tossed
over his shoulder before he closed the door.

The brandy decanter on the liquor cabinet drew him.
One glass, an easy chair and an open window were the
only scenery that interested him as he tried to piece together his thoughts. Her work bothered him more for her
sake than his own, he realized. He was afraid for her. It
was that simple and that complicated. Yet the very things
that attracted him to her were created and honed by the
profession she practiced so completely. He didn't want to

admit what he felt. He also didn't want to admit that he was as caught up in the possibility of catching the Island thief as he had ever been on the most intriguing architectural challenge he had faced. That fitted neither his lifestyle nor the image he had had of himself for so long.

Like Lacy, it would seem he had a weakness for puzzles. And in this puzzle he had a stake. His godmother would have been enough on her own, but Lacy was a bonus he had not thought to encounter. Where they were going he had no idea. How they would get there was just as unknown. But one thing was for certain: the road would be as twisted as that crazy case that had drawn Lacy into the maze of detective work to begin with. It had to be. Anyone who could keep a kitchen in a minor state of chaos, carry a gun around as though it was a toy and dig into the criminal mind to find answers, was guaranteed to challenge the most stick-in-the-mud mentality ever created. Namely his.

Eight

Lacy paced the kitchen, resisting the urge to peer out the window. David should be arriving at any moment, and she was more nervous than she'd been in a long time. She was also irritated with herself for being in such a state. She kept trying to tell herself that David was only a man, a sexy male she wanted to go to bed with. What could be simpler?

But nothing was simple where David was concerned. It was more than an uncomplicated desire that made her want to look her best. It was more than passion that made her wish she could understand the man. It was more than a biological function that made her feel good just being in the same room with him. It was more than sex appeal that made her laugh and forget the ugliness of some of the things she had seen in her life.

The sound of a car pulling into her parking area caught her attention. David. She froze for an instant. The mem-

ory of the way he had left her the night before came viv-
idly to mind. The doorbell rang. She took one step, then
two. She couldn't refuse to let him in, she reminded herself as she walked the rest of the way down the hall. She
could handle the awkwardness. She was an adult.

"Ready?" David asked the moment she opened the
door. His gaze slipped over her, taking in every detail of
the aqua slacks, topsiders, and white-and-aqua striped
oversize shirt. A darker blue cardigan was tied by the
sleeves around her shoulders. She looked fashionable,
downright sexy and good enough to eat. He smiled as he
stepped forward to span her waist with his hands.

"What are you doing?"

"Collecting my morning kiss," he murmured before
dipping his head to do just that.

To say that Lacy was surprised at his actions would
have been an understatement. Her lips parted in a small
O of astonishment. It was all the leeway David needed.
Before she knew what was happening he took possession
of her mouth in a kiss that would have boiled water. For
one second Lacy thought of resisting. Then she mentally
threw up her hands and decided to take what was offered and ask questions later. There comes a time when
any smart woman knows to shut up and enjoy.

And enjoy she did. From the first touch of his tongue
to the glide of hands across the burgeoning fullness of her
breasts as they swelled in anticipation. Had she thought
him sexy? She should have added illegal. Erotic images
filled her mind, heating her blood and softening her body
to mold to his. Her hands were as busy as his, stroking,
exploring the contours and planes that made them glo-
riously different.

"We should close the door," David whispered against
her lips.

"What door?"

"The one leaving a draft against my back."

Disengaging one hand reluctantly from the eager feminine flesh that seemed created to fit in his palm, David slammed the door. "I was a fool last night," he said hoarsely. He wanted her too much not to clear the air before he tasted her passion.

"I should have told you," Lacy added, willing to take half the blame. "Is it all right now?" For the moment the desire within was leashed to allow for the words that needed to be said. She had to know he wouldn't turn away this time.

Their eyes met, each asking a silent question of the other. "I won't pretend your work doesn't bother me. It does." His hands caressed her back as he spoke. "The risks you take worry me. It doesn't make sense to you perhaps. I care," he added finally, no longer prepared to go slow. He wanted her to know what he felt.

The effect of his admission on Lacy was more than she'd bargained for. Two small words. They touched her in a way she had never been touched before. She was familiar with the word *want*. Care was one she didn't know. Less than love, yet more than desire; more even than she had expected.

Lacy lifted her hand to his cheek. "I understood," she murmured.

"Did you?" He searched her face, seeing the truth written there. "I don't think I'll ever be comfortable with it, you know."

Ever had such a permanent ring to it. Lacy almost, but not quite, said as much. "Don't think about it. I don't."

"Somehow I thought you would say that." The sadness that tugged at his heart shocked him. That she would close the door on the reality of her world bothered him, yet he would say no more. He had no right. Her life was her choice. Not his.

He gathered her close to blot out the feelings inside. To hold Lacy he would have to forget his reservations and live the way she did. "We have an hour or so that we could kill," he whispered suggestively. There would be no pulling back this time for either of them.

"Do we?" Lacy smiled as he bent his head and took her lips, sharing her smile. She had thought she'd meet the gentle tender lover she had known. Instead she found her senses drowning in a man's deep need. He held her close, his body imprinting itself on her with every breath she drew. His mouth took hers, his tongue slipping in to drink of her as though he were thirsty and she were water in the desert.

David took all that she would give and more. The male in him was intent on staking his claim, of teaching this woman the meaning of his desire, his passion. Without breaking the kiss he lifted her in his arms. "There is no turning back," he warned in a deep voice as he started up the stairs to her bedroom.

"I know," she whispered, delighting in the way he held her.

Once upstairs, David set her on her feet beside the bed, his hands lingering over her curves before he began to slip the sweater from her shoulders.

"I can do it."

He shook his head. "Next time, if you like. Not now."

Her shirt, slacks and shoes followed the way of the sweater, leaving her clad in tiny bikini panties of flesh-colored lace and silk and an even smaller bra.

David's eyes burned with need as he undressed her. Lacy watched him with the same intensity that he felt, her eyes clouding with the desire his caresses created in her.

She faced him honestly, neither hiding nor preening as he
stroked her length slowly. His eyes held hers as he shed
his clothes. To look away was impossible. He saw the
passion weigh her lashes. He watched the appreciation
grow in her eyes as more of his body was revealed to her.

"Woman, you are something else," he breathed,
coming to her.

She moved into his arms, delighting in the way he
pulled her down on the bed. "For you, I want to be."

David lifted her on top of him, his hands caressing her
face. She was so beautiful, her hair cascading to his chest
to wrap them in an inky veil. "I want you so much."

Lacy felt the slight shaking of his fingers, the first sign
of vulnerability she'd seen in him. She gazed into his eyes,
pleased to know he was as affected by her as she was by
him. David drew an unsteady breath at her look. He
reached out to gently cup the warm silk of her breast.
Admiration flowed in his touch as he stroked the full
curve. His lips anointed each peak with the lightest of
kisses, bringing a gasp of aching pleasure to Lacy's
throat.

Lacy trembled in his arms, the yearning inside her
twisting higher. "Touch me," she pleaded in a husky
throb, arching to meet his mouth as it hovered so near
and yet so far.

David shook his head, each motion stirring a faint
whisper of air across her skin. "There's no rush."

His thumbs slowly stroked her nipples as Lacy responded eagerly to his ministrations and the evocative
effect of his words. She looked at him while he touched
her, reveling in the rapt expression on his face. Her hand
slipped between their bodies and she found him, cradling him in her palm.

"I want you to love me," she whispered in a velvety voice. She sank deeper into his body, needing the heat of him to surround her. Drawing her breasts across his lightly furred chest, she teased him the way he did her.

A violent shudder shook him as she writhed over him. She pressed kisses along the straight line of his shoulder, her tongue flicking out to tease and taste his flesh. She lifted herself, working her way up his throat to the edge of his jaw. She was so engrossed in her exploration and the satisfaction she got with every response that she lost all thought beyond the feel of his body against hers, his hands molding her to him.

David captured Lacy's lips. He had allowed her the freedom to touch him long enough. It was his turn now. His tongue invaded her mouth with hot urgency, exploring and playing with her own until they were consumed with mutual hunger. Lacy inhaled sharply as her body quivered with desire. Leisurely, David nibbled his way down her soft skin, turning them so that she lay on her back beneath him. He placed a hand on the gentle swell of her belly and began a slow massage that had her arching ardently against his heated touch. Lacy was going insane wanting him.

Each touch was a galvanic shock. Each teasing bite fed a fever that created a molten ache that touched every part of her. Lacy's breath came in light pants between her parted lips. Moans born of unappeased desire grew in her throat.

David raised his head, his expression mirroring his almost savage pleasure. He smiled into her passion-dark eyes before resuming his tormenting love play.

Lacy bit her lip in frustration at the maddening pace of his teasing arousal. Even in her highly charged state she recognized his tactics. Part of her rejoiced in his obvious need to make her his, yet her strength demanded she also take him as her own. Lacy caught his shoulders, unconsciously digging her nails into him with the urgency of her demand.

Lacy's lips curved into a wicked smile as he moved to reposition himself to possess her. She closed her legs, capturing him in her soft warmth. At the same time, she turned until David rolled on his back with her on top.

She moved over him, taking tiny bites of his shoulder, his throat. Making her way down his body she tasted his skin, pleasuring him as he had her. His muscles knotted with tension as she slowly slipped across his stomach. She sipped at the well of his navel until he arched toward her with a wild groan deep in his throat.

"Enough," he ordered thickly. His hands captured her, cupping under her breasts to lift her in position above him. With a hard, driving thrust he plunged into her.

Her head thrown back, Lacy abandoned herself to the fiery rhythm he set. His hands caressed every inch of her, stroking, kneading, possessing. Tension mounted in her, deliciously filling every particle of her being. Heat flowed through her, fusing her body to his, driving them toward a white-hot climax.

Twisting, turning, each muscle straining for the peak coming ever closer. Just when Lacy knew she could stand no more, David thrust them up and over in one powerful surge. Tension shattered into fragments. Two names rose as one. Two people held onto each other as though the earth trembled in a convulsive quake. The aftermath was as deep and as rich as their passion had been. They lay entwined, silenced and satiated.

For one moment there had been no his world, no her world. Only their world existed.

Lacy was the first one to stir. Her lashes lifted, her hands slowly savored the solid muscles beneath her cheek. The scent of lovemaking was heavy in the air. She inhaled it, committing the sweet fragrance to memory.

"Wow!" David murmured huskily. There was so much he wanted to say but he knew it was too soon. Lacy was still wary. She still needed to believe she was in control. He had her body but he wanted more.

Lacy smiled, her tongue flicking out to lick up a droplet of perspiration. The tang of salt and male was pleasant in her mouth. "I think I've heard that comment somewhere before."

David lifted a hand to smooth the hair back from the face she raised to his. His fingers were shaking, he realized absently. "You are wonderful."

"You're not so bad yourself."

David searched her expression, finding satisfaction, lingering desire and the slight weariness that always seemed to haunt her eyes. He frowned.

Lacy saw the small change, her eyes narrowing to the probing look that had become so much a part of her. "What's wrong?"

David shook his head, forcing his expression to reveal all she expected to see. "Nothing. I was just trying to decide if I dare try to talk you into forgetting about sailing today. The ocean is a bit rough." The half-truth slipped off his tongue as though it had been waiting there for him to use.

"We could go up the St. Lucie River." Lacy made her suggestion absently while trying to decide if he was really thinking of their trip or something else.

"Would you like that?" Questions. They always caught her attention. How glad he was that he knew the key to sidetracking that perception of hers. She still didn't fully understand his concern, despite what she said.

Lacy grinned, her interest piqued. "I would like anything that would get me out on the water. It's been too long since I had a real day off." And more importantly, she would welcome the time alone with David. If they didn't do anything more than find a secluded cove and anchor up, she would be content just to be with him.

"You mean we aren't going crook hunting today?" David couldn't resist planting a kiss on the tip of her nose. It was either tease her or make love to her again.

Lacy wrinkled the saluted feature. "That makes me feel about ten years old."

"Good." He rose, pulling her with him. "We're going to play like ten-year-olds for the day. It's a bit too cold to swim, but I had my cook pack a picnic and I picked out a bottle of wine. We'll cruise around, sun a little, maybe even take a nap."

Lacy slipped out of his arms, tossing him a wicked smile. "Nap as in sleep, or nap as in afternoon games?" She padded across the room to the adjoining bath. David was right on her heels.

"Nap as in sleep. No one but a contortionist would be able to make love on a narrow bunk like the ones in my twenty-footer. Besides, the nap idea was only a throwaway line. I don't really want to waste any of our time together sleeping." He reached into the shower to turn on the tap.

Lacy stared at him. It hadn't occurred to her that he would join her. Not that she minded, she decided, when he gently urged her into the stall. A second later she discovered the major benefit of showering with a friend. Soapy masculine hands were infinitely suited to washing the female body. Long, slow strokes reached the length of her legs. Warm, wet palms cupped her breasts, circling the peaked nipples before slipping up the sides of her throat to the whorls of her ears. Chills of sensations merged with the pleasantly hot spray pouring down her back. Her bones had all the consistency of warm taffy. Lacy sagged against David's body, sighing when his arm wrapped around her waist to support her while the other hand kept up the slow caressing cleansing.

By the time David was done she was past caring whether she was clean or not. She was barely aware of him wrapping her in a towel and carrying her to bed once again. Her whole being was centered on him, the feel of his body surging against her own. His name was on her lips as once more she followed him to the peak of desire and beyond. His hands were buried in her hair when she opened her eyes to find him staring at her face as though he would memorize every feature.

"David?" So much lay in the silvery depths of his eyes. So many emotions, some she was afraid to identify. "Don't look at me like that."

"Like what, Lacy?" It was almost impossible to hold back the questions clamoring for release. How could she give herself to him so freely? How could she place her career before the passionate woman who lived within the person who studied, probed and searched for solutions to puzzles? How could she not see how much he cared?

"Like you want more than I have to give." The words slipped out, carrying a desperation she hadn't realized lived within her.

David shut his eyes for an instant, caught in the words he had said too often in the past. "How do you know you don't have more to give until you try. Trust me a little. Trust yourself enough to risk reaching out." Lifting his lashes, he saw the confusion that slipped across her expression for a second.

"I trust you. How can you think I don't?"

He laughed shortly, almost grimly at yet another question. Weren't there enough of those without her adding more? "Is this all you want from me?" He returned her question with one of his own.

"It's all we can expect. Can you honestly see the two of us together, merging your life with mine? I know next to nothing about your work. All we've done is talk about mine. And that, you tolerate for me and the charade."

At the word charade, David felt anger stir within him. He rolled so that he pinned her to the bed. "This is no charade. It never has been. I'm not someone you can take up with and then put down when this job is over. And you aren't the kind of woman who indulges in casual sex, so don't pretend you are."

"What do you want?" Lacy lay still, imprisoned by her desire to see inside his mind, to understand what he would have of her.

David hesitated, not immediately having the exact words to reply. "I want more than a quick affair," he said at last, giving the only answer he knew for certain.

"That leaves a lot of ground untouched," Lacy murmured, not sure how she felt at that moment. She hadn't thought about tomorrow. She'd been afraid to.

"Just give us a chance. Don't back off before we try to be more than this." He waved his hand to encompass the intimacy of their position.

"We don't match," she protested, seeing nothing but hurt down the road for both of them.

"I know." His agreement was as realistic as her protest. "But I'm willing to risk it. Are you?"

The blatant challenge was unexpected. The fact that David had used it showed his knowledge of her. Lacy wasn't certain in that moment whether to be glad or sorry that he read her so well.

"And if I hurt you?"

"How like you not to worry about yourself. Most women would, you know." He pulled her tight against him, fitting her body to his. He wanted her agreement more than he had wanted anything in a long time, but he knew when to back off. If he pushed too hard she would run. He had her confused. It was enough for now.

"You're crazy," Lacy said on a half laugh.

David wasn't about to be sidetracked. "Say it, Lacy."

"All right, we'll play it your way," she agreed, realizing he wouldn't give up. His determination was every bit as strong as her own.

His kiss was quick and hard, carrying relief and passion. "You won't be sorry. I promise."

"We'll see."

He lifted his head. "Now don't go getting cold feet on me." He dared to tease.

Lacy pushed at his chest. "Stop baiting me. It's not polite to treat the woman you just made mad, passionate love to that way."

David stared at her as though she had sprouted wings and a halo. "You made a joke." He had taught her that, had shown her how to laugh, to have fun over nothing.

Lacy slipped off the bed and gathered her clothes. "And we are going to be late if you don't get a move on."

David lay there for a moment, enjoying watching her. Her body was still warm from his possession, her skin glowed with remnants of passion. She had been his and she would be again. "I was hoping we could stay here."

Lacy was tempted, so very tempted. But they needed to make an appearance at the Island's boat dock. Each time she and David were seen publicly was one more scene in the charade they had to play. She didn't want her job to touch their day but it must, for a short time. "No way. We have work to do, remember?"

"I remember, but I wish I didn't," David muttered beneath his breath.

He was still wishing they could have stayed at her town house when they arrived at the Island yacht club where his weekender was docked. Twenty feet of cramped boat had sounded good yesterday, but today its limitations were too much. Yet, looking at Lacy's laughing face as she exchanged greetings with the people who hailed them as they walked down the dock, made him glad he had thought to invite her.

"Ahoy, David!" Jeffrey Osgood came out on deck of a sleek cabin cruiser, a coffee cup in hand. "Come aboard. Charles just made a fresh pot." He paused, staring at Lacy for a minute, clearly trying to place her. "Aren't you the lady who came to talk to us about the theft?"

Lacy squeezed David's arm, silently signaling him to accept the invitation. "I am. That's how I met David," she added, giving the younger Osgood her best wide-eyed look. She felt David's surprise at her tactics, although nothing in his expression betrayed his opinion.

"A cup or two would hit the spot. It's a bit nippy out here," David commented lightly, helping Lacy aboard. If she intended to play the carefree, smitten female then he would do his part. The Osgoods, uncle and nephew, weren't close friends but they were amusing. And if it would help Lacy solve the burglaries he would have weathered even the most dreary of his acquaintances.

Charles appeared in the doorway of the cabin, a welcoming smile on his face. It faltered slightly on seeing Lacy, then re-formed when he realized her presence was strictly social. It only took a few minutes for them to sort themselves out, each cradling a mug of fresh-brewed coffee, and to sit down in the spacious salon. The intracoastal gleamed like a deep blue mirror beyond the wide expanse of windows on the port side.

"It is beautiful here." Charles nodded to the sparsely populated opposite bank. "You know, until I retired I never had time to boat or enjoy myself by just being lazy."

Jeffrey snorted. "I don't think I would call your life lazy by any stretch of the imagination. And don't pretend you like being retired, either. Why only last night you were grumbling about how bored you were."

Clearly displeased at the insertion, Charles shook his head. "Did I say 'bored?' I should have said 'let down.' I had just finished that metal project, didn't I tell you?"

Jeffrey stared at him for a moment. "No, you didn't."

Curious, Lacy asked, "What metal project?"

Charles turned to her. "I took up working with small tools and various metals. I needed something to do with my time now that Jeffrey has the business." He paused long enough to shoot his relative a look that held a mixture of frustration and resignation. "Actually, my doctor suggested it about the time he told me I had to slow down or my hypertension would catch up with me," he added in a slightly milder tone.

"Now uncle," Jeffrey chided, giving his relative a look that was less affectionate than his tone. "This is too nice a day to be discussing your health. You know you've never felt better in your life. You've told me so, often enough in the past few weeks." He turned to Lacy and

David. "I was beginning to despair of him ever settling down to the slower pace of the Gold Coast."

"There's precious little slow about this area," Charles pointed out. "In case you haven't noticed this place is in the middle of a building boom. We're lucky a group of us had the foresight to purchase that land across the way when we did. We'd be smack in the middle of a shopping mall by now otherwise."

"Maybe it wasn't as good an idea as you think. Has it occurred to you that if there had been some development across the intracoastal the thief who's plaguing us would have a lot more difficulty in waltzing in and out without anyone seeing him? You wouldn't be minus your Gold Lady and the rest of the victims would still have their heirlooms."

"Since when have you cared about heirlooms. All you see is modern," Charles muttered irritably. "You can't begin to understand how Clara and the Graysons feel about their treasures."

"I know, Uncle," Jeffrey tried to placate his relative. "I can't help it that I prefer modern things to the old."

Charles harrumphed irritably before remembering that they had guests. "I am sorry, my dear." He reached across to pat Lacy's hand. "It just makes me so angry to think that someone could circumvent our security without so much as a 'by your leave' and take off with anything that takes his fancy. What is the world coming to?"

David downed the rest of his coffee without haste, but with definite purpose. Giving Lacy's knee a squeeze beneath the table, he got her attention. "We'll be on our way now."

Lacy smiled, wondering what David was playing at. She still had questions she wanted to ask, but she followed his lead anyway. Something was up. She could feel

tension in the thigh pressed against hers. David had some
bit of information. She knew it but hadn't an idea of
what it could be. His arm was stiff around her waist as he
guided her toward the mooring slip at the end of the
dock.

"You know, sweetheart, I think it's rougher than
would be pleasant. Are you sure you want to go out?"

The slightly raised voice, the obvious endearment and
the warning look in David's eyes were clues too blatant
to be ignored.

"What I would really like to do is window-shop for a
bit. I hardly ever get the chance," she said, playing the
scene he had set for them.

"Are you sure?" David turned her in his arms. The
public demonstration was out of character for him, but
he didn't think the Osgoods would know that.

"Positive."

He dropped a light kiss on Lacy's lips. "I'll explain in
the car," he whispered before lifting his head. "Then
window-shopping it is," he said in a normal tone for the
benefit of anyone who might be listening.

Nine

"All right. What gives?" Lacy demanded, as soon as David got in the car beside her.

He started the engine before answering. How did he explain the hunch he had? "Something Charles said about heirlooms bothers me," he admitted slowly. "Did you notice anything strange about the list of things stolen from my godmother's house?"

Frowning, Lacy shook her head. She knew better than to think the questions unrelated. "I don't think so," she replied, searching her memory.

"My godmother only has one heirloom with her down here. And that's the Dellwood family emerald. Everything in her home is new or modern. When she had me design that house she specifically requested that it be as sleek and as new-Florida as possible. Her exact words were 'I may be growing older by the day, but I don't have to live my whole life surrounded by antiques.'" He took his eyes from the road long enough to glance at Lacy. "Her home in Maryland is a showplace, and when she's not in residence it's even open to the public. There is only one way anyone could mention Clara and heirlooms in the same sentence, and that's to know that she keeps the emerald in the safe of whatever house she is in. As far as I know, no one but the family is privy to that information."

"But there was no mention of a missing emerald on the list of stolen property. I would have remembered." Lacy stared at him. "Are you trying to say that the Osgoods know something about the robberies? That the emerald was stolen and your godmother doesn't know about it?" she demanded, struggling with the idea.

"I don't know. What I do know is that everyone who knows Clara is aware of her preference for the modern, at least here. She hasn't made any secret of it over the years. And she and Charles are very good friends."

"Maybe heirloom was just a figure of speech," she offered.

"It could have been. I want to be sure. I want to see if that emerald is still in the house. Clara would have notified me if she had known it was missing."

Lacy frowned. "Why? What's so special about the emerald? Other than the obvious of course?"

"It's mine, or will be when I marry. Clara would never have kept its disappearance a secret. Especially not from me."

Lacy was prey to two different and distinct emotions. One had no place in the moment. She would not let herself recognize or admit the unexpected pain that his future with another woman would cause. Her personal feelings had no right to exist when she was faced with what could be the first break in this case.

The second emotion was a rising excitement. It was time they had a lead. So far all she had done was work over ground others had tramped before her. This was virgin territory.

"I take it we're on our way to see your godmother," she said after a second.

"We are. I just hope she's home." David was thinking, too. A lot of things were adding up. Little pieces of gossip about the Osgoods.

"I hate having to bother your relatives again. The robbery hit them so hard," Lacy murmured, remembering how upset the two older women had been.

David glanced at her, his expression softening at the look in her eyes. "I wish I could understand how you do the work that you do and still stay as sensitive to others as you are. You're marshmallow soft."

Lacy grimaced, shooting him a look that was anything but soft. "Don't you believe it," she warned, stiffening despite herself. This was the one thing she had fought since she had entered John's firm. It was also the trait that John had warned her about. She couldn't afford to be soft. She had to be tough or at least look the part. She had never been able to completely achieve the first, but she had perfected the second so that only she knew for sure. Until David came along and found her out.

She was withdrawing from him again. David could feel it. He spoke, saying the words calculated to pull her back, if only to answer a challenge. "I believe it, enough to offer to break the news to my godmother," he returned, watching her closely despite having half his attention on his driving.

Lacy thought that over. From someone else she would have resented the idea, but from David she found it easy to see the good sense in what he offered. Their suspicions would come as a shock to Clara Dellwood whether the emerald was missing or not. David would be better equipped to deal with that than she. As for the questions, her lover had an amazing grasp of the situation. And he could be trusted to get the answers needed. With that realization came the knowledge that this was the first time ever she had turned even a small part of her authority over to another person. She had never trusted anyone but her uncle enough, and he would have refused to accept the task unless she had been in desperate need. John had taught her self-sufficiency, but David was teaching her a much more important lesson: how to share.

"All right," she said quietly.

David gave her a sharp look. He hadn't expected her capitulation without an argument. Satisfaction filled him that she was finally beginning to reach out to him.

Clara and her sister were just on their way into lunch when Lacy and David arrived. The two women greeted their unexpected visitors with pleasure, inviting them to join them at the table.

"No, thank you, Godmother," David replied, taking the older woman's hand in his. "Lacy and I aren't here on a social visit."

Clara stared at him, her lined face paling slightly at the serious tone. "You aren't?"

David shook his head. He hated to upset her, but it had to be done. "It's about the theft."

"They've found the thief." Clara clutched his fingers, a smile beginning to form on her lips. It died on seeing the slight shake of David's head.

"No. Far from it, I'm afraid." He led her to a chair.

Lacy moved toward Alicia, ready to support the woman if the information that came next was too much for her.

"There is no easy way to say this, Godmother. I wish there was." He paused, searching for words that would not come. The emerald was a prized piece of their family's history and Clara was keeper of the heirloom. Knowing his relative, Clara would blame herself for its loss. "Was there anything missing that you didn't tell the police about?" he asked carefully.

Clara stared at him, her brow wrinkled in puzzlement. "I don't know what you mean," she replied after a moment of thought.

"Did you check the safe, your jewel box?"

"I checked my jewel box and the safe though I didn't want to. You know the problems I always have with that combination. But the police would insist. Nothing was gone, I assure you."

"Are you positive? Did you open all the cases?"

Clara started to nod, then stopped. "Well no, not all. Nothing had been touched, you see. The nice man who helped me told me that. At least I think he did, but I was so upset...." Her voice trailed off, her eyes rounding with comprehension. "You think that something else is gone, don't you. What? Tell me." She gripped his hands tightly.

David couldn't bring himself to placate her when it was very possible in the next few minutes they would all see the emerald was gone. "I think the Dellwood emerald may be among the missing."

Clara pressed her free hand to her lips, looking horrified. "No! No! It can't be," she whispered.

Alicia seconded her opinion although with slightly less shock. Lacy took the hand the older woman unconsciously held out for comfort. "We can't be certain," Lacy murmured, trying to be fair.

David glanced at her, making her wish she hadn't spoken. "I'll check," he said firmly, releasing Clara to get to his feet.

"We'll all check," Clara decided, jumping up. The determination in her expression stopped any objection David might have made.

"As you wish, Godmother," he replied before leading the way to Clara's bedroom.

Lacy followed Alicia up the stairs, wishing for the Dellwoods' sake that the emerald was not a victim of the thief. The safe revealed nothing out of the ordinary. None of the very expensive jewels appeared to have been touched. The velvet boxes were lined up according to size. Each case was opened, then closed again when found filled. It was only the last, the faded blue velvet case with the worn gold edge, that was different. David opened it slowly. All eyes were on his hands.

Alicia's cry was barely softer than Clara's. The words were nearly identical. "It's really gone!"

David raised his gaze from the empty box he held to stare at Lacy. The two sisters crowded around him, reaching out to touch in disbelief the place where once the ring had lain. The anger in his eyes was a fiery blaze. Lacy sympathized with him and the loss that clearly meant so much to his family.

"If there's any way possible we will get it back," she promised him. She could no more have stopped the words from leaving her lips than she could have stopped the tide. She wanted to comfort him, to hold him and take away the feeling of violation that one always knew when something was stolen.

"I'll settle for catching the man," he said quietly, but with a grimness no one but a fool could mistake.

With those words David turned his attention to his relatives. It was nearly an hour later before they were free to leave the house. The police had been notified about the new development although they hadn't been told how she and David had come to check the safe again. Clara and Alicia had been calmed and soothed.

"So what now?" David demanded. The need for action was paramount.

Lacy turned her head from the unseeing study she had been making of the road off the Island. "Now I go to the office and crank up the computers. There's not a lot I can do, but I can make a start. We need to know about the Osgoods. Crimes are committed with a motive. Maybe not always understandable, but always there. We have to find a reason why the Osgoods, one or both, would be involved, and that's assuming they are involved in the first place. Feel like helping me solve the puzzle?"

"Do you need to ask? I just sat in front of Chief Riley and lied my head off about why we thought to check the safe again. I wouldn't have done it if I wasn't becoming as determined and as curious as you." He looked at her and then back at the road. "It just doesn't make sense, as far as I know, for Charles or Jeffrey to be part of something like this. And if one of them isn't, how did Charles know about the emerald when no one else did?"

"We aren't sure he did know about the emerald. His comment could have been completely innocent."

"Do you believe that?"

"I don't disbelieve it." Lacy shrugged slightly. "Other things are beginning to bother me."

"Such as?"

"The metalworking he admits to. How good is he at it? Could he reproduce the keys? And if he could, how does he get his hands on the originals long enough without anyone realizing they are gone? And what about the fact that until a few weeks ago he had been grousing about being bored, and suddenly he stopped?"

"Maybe his hobby is responsible," David murmured.

"Perhaps. But equally possible is that he found something else to occupy his mind."

"As for his skill, I'd say that if a man like Charles took up something he'd be better than good at it."

"And the opportunity?"

David frowned, considering the possibility. "In Clara's case the answer has to be yes," he admitted. "He runs tame in her house. As for the Graysons? I don't know."

"He was at the club the day the Graysons and a group of their friends decided to go to Fort Lauderdale the night of the robbery. He was invited to accompany them, but he didn't."

"But he was a victim, too," David pointed out, trying to be fair.

"Could have been a smoke screen. His house is also in a very interesting position. Have you noticed?"

Fortunately, a stoplight turned red just at the second David made the connection. "All the residences are in a straight line. Grayson, Osgood, Dellwood—" he paused, then finished in a softer tone "—and mine."

"And yours," she agreed quietly.

"I just can't figure Charles as the thief."

"I can't either. On the surface I agree it doesn't make sense. Why take things that are so distinctive? Why steal and then not try to dispose of the goods? None of this stuff has hit the streets yet. Why? Revenge? A prank? Need? Greed? What's this guy thinking while he outwits us all? Is he playing a game with us? A kind of catch-me-if-you-can crook?''

David said nothing. Lacy's questions had no answer for either of them, only more questions, more trails to follow. They finished the drive to Lacy's office in silence. David entered, looking around the place where she worked, carefully. It was his first visit to the agency, not that there had been time before this. What he saw surprised him a little. He hadn't realized he had been expecting something out of a Hollywood soundstage. If he had been in the mood he would have smiled at the unconscious image he had of what Lacy did. There was nothing in the building that couldn't have belonged to almost any business office anywhere. Desks without clutter, a tasteful, even elegant decor, and small offices opening off a center hall created the Tipton Detective Agency. The only unusual feature of the whole was a computer system that looked as if it could do everything but stand on its head.

David watched silently as Lacy took a seat before a terminal in her office and booted it on-line. "I don't know how you expect to do anything on Sunday," he was moved to point out.

Lacy lifted her head, long enough to give him a strange look. "I know some people and some things that aren't exactly illegal, but . . .''

He nodded once. Now she was working in the gray area that he had imagined. Sitting down, he watched her start punching in numbers. The concentration on her face closed him out, and yet he felt no loss. He was too caught up in the hunt, in the woman who sat beside him. If there was an answer he had every faith that Lacy would find it. It could have been minutes or hours later when Lacy finally refocused on him.

"I have gone as far as I can today. Tomorrow I can get more complete information."

"And?" David asked, forcing himself not to jump in with a dozen queries.

"And, there's nothing in Charles's history as far as I can tell that would explain or indicate that he's the thief."

"If not him, then who?" A second after he spoke he realized she had not included Jeffrey in her comment.

"Jeffrey?" Lacy's brows were silent punctuation marks to the lone word.

David stared. He hadn't really considered the younger Osgood as a suspect. "But why? As far as I know the man is as wealthy as his uncle, perhaps more so. And you heard him today."

"Yes, I heard them, and I also saw an older man and a very athletic younger one. Given the way our thief moves in, I think we should be looking at Jeffrey as strongly as Charles." She stared into space for a moment, then asked, "How well do you know either of them?"

"A little more than acquaintances and not quite as much as friends."

"What about habits? You know, things like gambling? Women? Expensive cars? The kinds of things that eat up money."

David thought carefully. "I think Jeffrey gambles a bit, but I've never heard that he's in over his head. The Osgood money is quite deep. It would be hard to reach the bottom unless the market took a nosedive. Until his retirement a year ago, Charles was very much a force to reckon with in the marketplace. Charles was and probably still is a chance-taker. He would invest in companies that had a slim-to-none success factor and then make a killing. Jeffrey is his exact opposite. Now that he is at the helm of the business the Osgood dealings are more conservative, but they're still making money hand over fist. No, I don't think it's the need for money that would drive either of them to pull this kind of stunt."

"Then you come up with a better guess."

David raked his fingers through his hair in frustration. He didn't have an explanation. "So now what? Do we just sit and wait for him to hit again?"

"We could stack the deck in our favor," Lacy offered slowly, half-thinking aloud. Her idea was farfetched, but she had tried and succeeded with crazier schemes.

"How?"

Lacy lifted her feet to the desktop and got comfortable. "How game are you?"

David's curiosity was aroused. "To do what, exactly?"

Lacy smiled slightly at the interest he made no effort to hide. If she had needed proof David had come to accept her work, she had it now. There wasn't a hint of rejection or reservation about whatever she might say. He was prepared to listen and reserve judgment until he had heard the whole.

"My uncle might call it a harebrained scheme."

"I have yet to know you to be anything approaching harebrained," David responded, with a faint grin. "So quit stalling."

Caught, Lacy didn't try to deny the charge. "So far we have a few constants. One, our man gets in and out of a security system that's very tight. Two, he takes only small, costly items and ones that seem to have some sort of an attachment for their owners."

"Agreed."

"What if we set up a possible target? Gave our guy a hit he couldn't resist?"

David caught on quickly. "I don't have anything that would interest him."

"Are you sure?"

"We also need a way to force the man to perform to our timetable," David added, considering the plan and reconsidering which of his possessions would provide the temptation they needed. "The only thing I have that might work is a collection of nineteenth-century snuffboxes. Come to think of it I believe both the Osgoods have expressed an interest in it over the years." He frowned. "Odd. Jeffrey doesn't have much use for things of the past. I wonder why he offered to buy the whole lot from me? It wasn't too long ago, as I recall."

"That sounds like just what we need," Lacy said, excitement stirring within her. The adrenaline always flowed when she was onto a lead.

"When do we bait this trap of yours?" David asked, catching a bit of her enthusiasm.

"I want to run a complete check on both of them first thing tomorrow before we do anything."

"And if you don't find something?"

"Then you and I are going to take a real chance with your collection and hope we're smarter and quicker than our thief."

"What about your uncle? Will you tell him what you're up to?"

"I'll have to. How do you feel about coming to my place around six in the evening with a little moral support? John will be there. This isn't our usual way of operating, so there's no guarantee that he'll even agree to my idea."

"Is this legal?"

Lacy laughed humorlessly. "It's not illegal."

"All right, Lacy, what was so important and so secret that I had to meet you here?" John demanded, hardly waiting until he got inside Lacy's town house. "I assume this has to do with the Island burglaries."

Lacy gestured him to a seat. David had called to say he would be a little late, and it was left to her to outline their plan. "I may be onto something," she said bluntly, taking a seat across from him. She ignored the sharp look her uncle gave her. She had his full attention. "David and I were going sailing yesterday. We met the Osgoods at the dock and had coffee with them. In the course of the conversation Charles said something about the Dellwoods losing an heirloom. I didn't think too much about it at the time, but David did. It seems his godmother has this little quirk."

She went on to explain about Clara's all-modern Florida home. John listened attentively, frowning occasionally, but allowing her to complete the whole. He leaned back in his chair at the end of her report, staring off into space. The doorbell rang, signaling David's arrival. Lacy went to let him in. John waited only long enough to see David seated on the couch next to Lacy before he spoke.

"You're certifiably crazy. You have absolutely no proof. I'll grant you that it's as peculiar as Hades for Charles to mention the heirloom, but there're many possible explanations. The Osgoods, one or both, just don't have any motive."

"I know," Lacy sighed. "I ran a computer check on both men and came up empty. Jeffrey gambles a bit but he is well within his income. Charles has no vices at all that I could find."

"Wonderful!" John glared at his niece before surging to his feet to pace to the window and then back. "And these are the people you're planning to trap. Not only is it just this side of legal, but if the police get involved it's entrapment, and you know that means no conviction when it goes to court." He inhaled deeply, his chest swelling with temper.

Her own temper rising, Lacy stood up, facing him with her hands on her hips. "David and I will set this up ourselves. We'll call the police if and when anyone takes the bait. That's not entrapment."

"It's a fool's errand," he stated flatly.

David watched the two Tiptons go at it. Neither was about to back down. "What have any of us got to lose?" he pointed out as they stood glaring at each other. "If nothing happens there is a good chance neither Osgood is involved, and if the trap is sprung we'll have our thief."

Two pairs of eyes swung in his direction. "The ethics," John objected.

"Exactly," Lacy exclaimed, giving David a grateful look. Budging John was an arduous process even under the best of circumstances. "It's time to try something."

"That's a rotten reason for doing anything," John muttered, slumping into a chair. For long minutes, no one spoke. Finally he raised his head to fix Lacy with a stern eye. "All right. I'll go along with this, but only if you play it safe all the way down the line. I know your propensity for skirting the edge of trouble."

Lacy hardly heard the condition. His agreement brought a relieved smile to her face and adrenaline singing in her blood. "It shouldn't take us long to set the stage. Four days at most."

Startled, David stared at her. "That soon?"

"There's no reason to wait."

John exchanged a glance with David. "See what I mean. Before you know it she has you involved in a tangle of plans."

"This isn't a tangle." Lacy pulled a notebook from her pocket and proceeded to outline her idea right down to the last detail. Before she was finished, both men had distinctly dazed eyes and awed expressions. "Simple," she commented, closing the pad with a small snap.

"It's simple all right," David agreed, just beginning to see what he was letting himself in for. "All I have to do is give my staff the night off, and manage to drop the information about the empty house and the fact that I am considering selling my collection. Hopefully that will prod the robber into making his move on our timetable, from a conversation that either includes the Osgoods or that I know will get back to them and then calmly walk out the door to hide in the bushes for who knows how many hours while I beat off the mosquitos with my bare hands."

If she had been in the mood, Lacy would have laughed at his expression.

John did, chuckling with as much gusto as he did everything in his life. "You can handle it," he murmured, enjoying seeing someone else on the receiving end of Lacy's Machiavellian plots. "Do you want to back out?"

David shook his head. "No way. If nothing else I mean to see how this ends." But more importantly he meant to be at Lacy's side, protecting her if need be. He had made her his, whether she admitted the claim or not.

Ten

———

What do you need that for?'' David demanded, watching as Lacy put on her holster.

Lacy glanced up, surprised at the question. "You don't expect us to wait around for our thief tonight without any form of protection, do you? There's a bad guy on the loose, in case you haven't noticed."

The flatness in her response came as a shock. David closed the distance between them, uneasy without knowing why. This was not the Lacy he had come to know. This creature resembled the one he had first seen stopped on the side of the road.

"What's wrong?" he asked, raising his hand to cup the side of her face.

Lacy shook her head slightly, having no definitive reply. "We'd better get out of here. Remember, you and I are supposed to be on our way to Fort Lauderdale for the evening."

David had picked her up at her home, taken her to the beach club and then brought her back to his house, ostensibly for after-dinner drinks before going on to their supposed destination. Both Jeffrey and Charles Osgood had been at the restaurant and had seen them. So far their plan was going beautifully. She should have been pleased, yet all she really wanted was for the evening to be over.

David stopped her when she would have moved away. "Answer me, Lacy." When she started to protest, he silenced her with a look. "We have plenty of time, and we're not going anywhere until you tell me what's wrong. What put that defeated look in your eyes again?"

"That's not defeat, it's disgust," she admitted briefly, cornered. Her thoughts tumbled out in short sentences filled with anger and a kind of bitterness. "If this is one of the Osgoods, do you realize how stupid these crimes are? Both of them have everything they could possibly want or need. Why would either of them stoop to something like this? Someone could get physically hurt tonight. Does he care? Was his motive so important that it was worth the emotional damage brought on by the invasion of home and security?"

David stared at her, taken aback by the vehemence. Her reaction was too strong not to be based on more than the thefts. Suddenly the pieces of her life fit together in new and frightening ways. How long had she lived in this world that was slowly eating her alive? Hadn't John or anyone else noticed the toll her work was taking? Or didn't they care because she was so obviously good at what she did? He couldn't believe the last, for he had seen Lacy and her uncle together. No one but a fool could doubt their love and respect for one another.

"Perhaps he has a good reason if it is Charles or Jeffrey," he offered, not believing the possibility himself but needing to do something to ease her mind.

Lacy gave him a straight look. "And what might it be?" she asked cynically. "Ask a murderer why, and he'll tell you all manner of excuses. Any criminal will. Even the law-abiding write books to exonerate or explain away the wrongdoer. And what do you think the chances are that if it is Osgood, that he won't get off with the help of some high-priced lawyer and the oh-so-fair judicial system?"

Startled, David didn't say anything for a moment. He hadn't even thought of the legalities of the problem until now. Unfortunately, what Lacy suspected was probably all too true. The knowledge wasn't reassuring. For a moment he knew a touch of the frustration Lacy was feeling and had clearly felt too often in the past.

"That's not our problem," he murmured finally.

"Isn't it?" Lacy stepped back, breaking the contact between them. She had expected too much, and she wasn't being fair in demanding David provide answers that even society didn't have.

"Don't." David caught her shoulders, halting her withdrawal. "Talk to me. We've been too much to each other to pretend."

Lacy searched his face, looking for and getting the understanding she needed. "I've gotten out of the habit of sharing," she whispered, wanting to apologize for shutting him out but not knowing how.

David's hands softened, stroking now instead of holding. One more of Lacy's defenses was crumbling before his eyes. She was letting him into her mind, sharing more than just her body. "Talk to me," he commanded gently. "You don't really like this work, do

you?'' He took a big risk in voicing what he believed to
be the truth. She could retreat so fast he could lose her for
good.

Lacy opened her mouth to lie and suddenly knew she
couldn't do it. She had no idea how David could've figured out what she herself had just discovered. ''No,'' she
said so quietly that the words were almost inaudible. ''In
the beginning I wanted to help people. I was idealistic
enough to want to make a difference. I loved the challenge of it, too. I was too naive to realize what was in the
darkness of the other side of life.''

David folded her in his arms. The hurt in her voice cut
him to the heart. There was no way he could give her
back her idealism or her innocence, but he could hold
her, and if she would let him he would take her away
from anything that would hurt her again. ''I'm sorry,
love,'' he murmured against her hair. The scent of her
wrapped around him, reminding him of all they had
shared.

Lacy laid her head against his chest, accepting the
caring of his embrace without feeling pressured to give
anything in return. He understood when no one else had.
When she had allowed no one else to get close enough to
see the truth. He made her laugh, taught her the meaning of passion and gave her another focus for her life.
Her arms tightened around him, and emotion rose
within, startling her with its force. More than passion, the
feeling was mint new, stronger than she had ever known.

David held on to her, aware something was changing
between them. The desire, the tenderness and the need to
protect he felt for Lacy emerged in its real guise. Love!
He loved Lacy. The knowledge filled him with a sudden
need to tell her. Before he thought, his hand slipped to
her chin to lift her face. The instant he saw her expres-

sion he realized his error. She didn't need words and promises that might still force more than she thought she had to give. She needed him to love her in a way she could accept. They didn't have much time, but he would make it enough.

"I want you." He touched her lips lightly, tracing the shape of them, teasing her. "Come with me now. We have time. I promise."

Lacy had no defenses left. Desire went through her in shock waves that weakened her legs so that she leaned into David's strength. When he pulled her down on the soft carpet in front of the windows overlooking the water she groaned her need against his mouth. It didn't matter that they could not wait to reach the bedroom upstairs. It didn't matter that they had a rendezvous with a thief. All that she felt or knew was contained in one man: David. His hands molded her with gentleness and power, moving her to his will. His hips pressed against her, telling her exactly how much he wanted her. She shivered and cried out, twisting against him wildly. Her clothes, his, scattered like leaves in the wind until they both lay bare but for the heat the flesh-to-flesh fire created.

"Now, David," she pleaded.

"My Lacy," he breathed against her lips as he moved to complete the union they both craved.

He took her mouth and her body with the same smooth motion, becoming a part of her, melting her around him. Lacy arched toward him, taking him deep into her. He was hot, fitting her as closely as her skin. She smiled against his throat and murmured words without meaning, words born of her pleasure and desire.

David stroked her slowly, despite the need hammering inside him. He savored each tiny motion of their bodies, so perfectly matched. Lacy's legs shifted, circling his waist, binding her to him as though she would never let him go. His restraint slipped a notch. Her hungry seeking took his breath away. His control shattered. His woman wanted him deeply, passionately, mindlessly. He needed her, had to possess and be possessed. He moved faster, creating a driving, pulsing rhythm, holding nothing back. With each stroke, each instant of shaking pleasure, the tension built between them. She was quivering, crying out beneath him, and still he drove them higher. Then he felt the intimate pulses of her release all around him. A second later he arched, thrusting to the womb that was the cradle of life. He shuddered and arched again and again, giving of himself as deeply as she gave to him.

Lacy absorbed the weight of his body, welcoming the heaviness and the heat. The tremors of desire fulfilled racking her body demanded she find a haven in his arms. A breath of separation would have been too much in that moment as she lay beneath him.

For long, gentle minutes, David and Lacy lay spent in each other's arms, drifting slowly back to an awareness of where they were. David smoothed his lips against the tangled, ebony fall of Lacy's hair. He kissed her temple, her cheek, the sensitive inner curve of her ear, smiling when she shivered at the touch of his tongue on her skin. Her fingers moved down his back to the powerful muscles of his buttocks and beyond, tracing the curves and hollows with a gentle lover's touch. David groaned and tightened inside her, sending sensations streaking through flesh that was still caught in the aftermath of the passion they had shared. Caressing him lightly again, Lacy smiled to know he was as affected by their loving as she.

"Lacy, do you know what you're doing?" David asked, his voice low and husky. There was a touch of amusement, too, for he had seen the smile she had tried to hide. "So you would tease your man." He moved deeply inside her, stealing her breath. He drank Lacy's choked cry from her lips as his hips arched again. "Is this what you want, lovely Lacy?" The hunger for her still rode him, demanding one more taste, one more caress, one more kiss.

David saw the surprise in her green eyes, felt the clinging of her body as she instinctively sought to increase the gliding pressure of his intimate caress. Passion tightened in David, surprising him in turn. He had thought only to pleasure them both, but nature had other ideas, glorious ideas.

"David?" Lacy opened her eyes, feeling the desire build. "I thought men couldn't . . ."

"Apparently this one can . . . with this woman." David took her lips as he took her body. "My woman." The words were on his lips as he brought them to ecstasy yet again.

"We have to get dressed," Lacy murmured, when she could speak again.

"I know." David hugged her close one last time before he lifted himself away from her body. He rose and pulled her to her feet, stealing a kiss before he let her go. "In a way I wish we could forget the whole thing and just go away somewhere, alone."

Lacy bent to retrieve her clothes, unwilling even now to admit how appealing his idea sounded. She tried to remember she had a job to do when all she wanted was to lie in his arms.

"Come on, honey, let's get this show on the road," he murmured, seeing the unspoken wish she had tried to hide. He slipped an arm around her waist, wishing neither of them had been so quick to start dressing. One more kiss.

Lacy responded with all the depth of emotion within her. Her feelings might not have a name, but there was no doubting their strength. She held him to her, forestalling the future for one more moment.

David raised his head, watching her intently. Was she beginning to see more than a man who could make her laugh and touch her with desire? He hoped so. More than anything in his life he realized he wanted Lacy to stay with him, to love with him.

Lacy made herself smile. David looked so serious. She touched his face, tracing the curve of his lips. He had given her solace. She would give to him in return. "When this is over let's go back to my place."

David inhaled deeply at the light touch. "I like your style, honey," he said huskily before turning her toward the door.

Lacy sent him a wicked look over her shoulder. For the first time in her life, she faced the job ahead without striving to control herself and the situation. She was no less alert for the change. The lack of tension in the way she moved, the way she could tease even now with the trap already laid was a freedom she had never experienced. "I'll remind you of that at a more appropriate time," she replied with a small laugh.

"You do that." David locked the house, slipped his arm around her and walked her to the car that was parked a few feet away.

The plan was for them to appear to leave the grounds, thus giving the robber, if he was watching, the impression of clear sailing. They had arranged with John to meet at the Blowing Rocks Park. Someone from the agency would then take their car while John drove back through the Island, slowing down enough for them to slip back to David's home unnoticed. They would then hide in the shrubs close to the terrace windows that overlooked the intracoastal and await the thief. If all went well the culprit would appear sometime between midnight and three in the morning.

The plan worked perfectly. She and David were in place. The house behind them was in darkness, and the moon was playing hide-and-seek with the clouds. The scent of the sea water, and the sound of night creatures on the prowl were the only signs of life. One hour passed, then two. Three and four were just as peaceful as the first part of the watch.

David shifted against the tree trunk where he rested. Lacy was curled beside him, her head on his shoulder. Their hiding place gave a complete view of the water approach to the property, so there had been no need for them to split up, a fact for which David was profoundly grateful. Sound carried too well at night to allow for speech, so he had contented himself with holding Lacy. Stroking her had seemed too natural to be resisted, although he was careful to only pleasure them both without prodding the fires of passion between them into a full blaze.

Lacy watched the water, alert enough to be aware of everything that went on around her, but enjoying David's touch so much she hardly noticed the passing of time. Wrapped in his arms with the night enfolding them in a cocoon of silence seemed more a joy than the job it should have been. Sighing softly, she snuggled closer, feeling David's arms tightening around her instantly. She smiled in the darkness. She liked the feeling of possession his action gave her. The warmth of him against her side, the touch of his hands soothed and pleasured.

Her eyes scanned the intracoastal, continuously watching for that shadow that should not move. Suddenly, she felt David tense.

"Do you see it?" he whispered against her ear. He turned her head slightly to give her the correct angle.

It took a moment for Lacy to pick out the shadow moving where it shouldn't have been. She stiffened. A boat gliding along the bank, hardly more than a few feet from shore, moved toward them.

If they hadn't been watching so carefully, they would have missed it. Even now as the craft was brought to the beach there was no ripple, no sound of a wave slapping against wood to alert anyone of the alien presence. A shadow leaped from the boat to the shore, the pole he held making the jump easy and soundless. The man moved by them at a slow walk, his feet passing over the ground without a whisper of noise. David's eyes narrowed trying to decide which, if either, of the Osgoods he was. David couldn't tell. He rose as silently as possible, pulling Lacy to her feet. For one instant his arms tightened around her before he let her go. He didn't want her involved in this. He couldn't stop her, but he could make certain he was the first one in the house in case of trouble.

In seconds they stood just outside the door, listening intently. All was silent in the house. David touched her shoulder when she would have preceded him. He signaled that he would lead. Lacy raised her brows, ready to protest, but he gave her no chance. He slipped past her into the empty foyer. The snuffbox collection was in the study. A few steps down the deserted hall brought them to the door. The robber was trapped in the room unless he wanted to go through a window. The light switch was next to the door. David got it at the same moment Lacy blocked the exit behind him. Her hand was on the gun, but it wasn't drawn as the lights went on.

Charles Osgood whirled around, a snuffbox in his hand. Dressed all in black, he looked the part of the burglar he had become. He wore no weapon.

"I should have suspected a trap," he murmured, his silver brows drawn slightly together. He shrugged, then smiled faintly. "It would seem I am well and truly caught."

"Is that all you have to say?" David demanded, angry at the offhand way the man spoke. As far as he could see there wasn't an ounce of remorse in Osgood. Lacy had been right all along. He risked a quick glance at her, then wished he hadn't. Her eyes held that disillusionment that he hated. She watched Charles with a kind of resigned acceptance. Wishing he could comfort Lacy and knowing he couldn't, at least not now, made him even angrier. He returned his attention to Charles.

Charles shrugged again. "What would you like me to say? I could try a few excuses, but neither of you would believe me. Besides, I don't deal in lies. It was fun while it lasted. I certainly livened up an otherwise boringly repetitive season."

Lacy watched him but said to David. "One of us better call the police."

"You do it. I'll keep an eye on our thief." David glared at Charles. "Put the snuffbox back, then sit down with your hands behind your head."

"Is this really necessary? I'm not a true criminal, you know."

"If you aren't I'd like to know what is," David shot back as Lacy moved to the phone.

"You're wasting your time, David," Lacy said as she dialed Riley's number.

"All the police are going to do is fill out a mass of forms, and in a few hours I'll be back at home and my lawyer will be earning his retainer for a change," Charles pointed out, obeying David to the letter.

"You're probably right, which doesn't say a hell of a lot for our judicial system. But the fact remains we're going through the motions anyway. If nothing else, this night is going to cost you a packet of money and quite a bit of publicity, if I have to call the papers myself. The law may not get their piece of your hide, but I guarantee you that the people on this island won't be thinking of you as one of them any longer."

David continued to study Charles. "How did you manage to copy the keys, assuming that is how you were getting in? I know I didn't leave mine anywhere."

Charles actually smiled at the question. "That was really the easiest part. I used the men's locker room at the club. Most of us play golf at one time or another. A game takes quite a while to finish. All I had to do was lift the keys, make the impression and then go home and reproduce it. Since I had a Garrick system, I had an example, if not the exact fit to compare."

Lacy hung up the phone and rejoined David. David was curious about the mechanics, but she wanted to know the motive. "Was the challenge of it the only reason?"

Charles was pleased at their interest. "I missed the push and shove of business. Jeffrey didn't need my help, and besides the corporate world was as repetitive as retirement. I wanted something different."

If he had chosen another means to give himself plea-sure and excitement one might have felt sorry for the man. But Charles had chosen to take his amusement at others' expense. A crime with no weapon, no damage, no clues. "When had you planned to stop?" Lacy asked, curiosity taking hold.

Charles shrugged again. "I hadn't decided. When it became too easy, I guess."

"And the goods?"

"Is that the word for the stolen property?"

"It is." Lacy leaned against the doorjamb, knowing they had little to fear from Charles now. All she wanted was to turn him over to the police and leave with David. She wanted to forget this evening had happened. She wanted to lose herself in her lover's arms once more.

"I thought I would just see that it got back to the rightful owners when I was done."

"And the insurance that everyone would've been paid?" David demanded, not liking the calm with which both Lacy and Charles discussed the situation. He wanted Lacy out of this mess, away from this fool who didn't seem to care that he hurt people.

Charles waved a dismissive hand. "Could have been worked out. With money there's always a way."

Lacy shook her head. "And the victims?"

Charles was honestly surprised at the question. "They would have had their goods back."

Neither David nor Lacy had an answer for that. The sound of cars pulling into his driveway made David glance down the hall. The police, with Chief Riley in the lead, entered the house a few seconds later.

David looked at Lacy. "We'll be out of here soon," he murmured.

Lacy smiled faintly. "You aren't remembering the paperwork," she said with just a hint of amusement. That she could find anything humorous about the situation was a measure of David's influence.

He rewarded her with a grin, his fingers brushing her cheek in a chaste caress.

Charles watched from the couch, a small frown between his brows. "I had wondered if you two were playing a game," Charles mused aloud. "I see now that you were not."

Lacy glanced at him. "I don't play that kind of game," she said coldly, suddenly angry. Her relationship with David was no game, it never had been, she realized.

"There's no reason for the heat, my dear," he pointed out as the police filed into the room en masse.

"That's a matter of opinion, Osgood," Chief Riley inserted grimly, signaling one of his men to read Charles his rights.

David stayed beside Lacy as Riley took over, asking questions of them all. His expression gave little away as he listened to their explanation of the events of the evening. Finally, he gestured for the room to be cleared of everyone but himself, David and Lacy.

"You were luckier than you deserve," the chief said bluntly, staring at them. "What if you had been wrong?"

"We weren't and that's all that matters," Lacy pointed out wearily. "The thieving is over."

"You should have let me in on this," he added, not prepared to leave the situation alone.

"How?" David demanded. "Your hands are tied with more rules than Lacy had."

Riley rounded on him. "Someone could have been hurt. Lacy, you or Osgood. Then where would any of us have been?"

Lacy sighed deeply. "Is there really any point to this?" she asked of no one in particular. "It's done now and everything turned out fine. Can't we just leave it at that?"

Riley opened his mouth to say more, but David beat him to it. "Good idea, honey. It's been a long night. Let's get you home." He slipped an arm around Lacy's waist before looking hard at Riley. "That is unless you have any more questions for us?" One brow kicked up as he challenged the older man. The power of his name and family was behind him, and for the first time in his life he used both to gain what he wished.

Riley heard the subtle threat and slowly inclined his head. He was a realist. "I don't like your methods, but I'm glad they succeeded," he said finally, moving away from the door.

"I wasn't too thrilled with them, either," Lacy admitted as they started to leave. "I'm sorry I couldn't have told you our plans in advance."

At her words, Riley's grim expression eased somewhat. A small inclination of his head was all he allowed himself as they passed. David guided Lacy through the house and out the door without speaking. He purposely didn't look at the patrol car in which Charles sat. He did, however, watch Lacy. She paid no attention to the man she had brought to justice, either. Instead she seemed lost in thought, hardly noticing when he urged her into the car. Silence wrapped around them as he drove back to her town house. David glanced at her, more concerned with each passing mile.

"Are you all right?" he asked at last.

Lacy turned her head, then nodded. "A little tired."

Relieved she was talking, David murmured, "I'm not surprised. It's after four in the morning." He pulled to a stop in front of her place.

"You are coming in, aren't you?" She needed him more than she could say. In the past she would have wanted to be alone after a night like this one. But not now. She wanted David beside her, holding her, making her believe there was truth and light still in the world, that laughter was stronger and more enduring than pain and suffering.

David frowned at the almost desperate tone in her voice. Anger re-formed in him at the toll the night had taken on her. Damn Osgood, he swore silently. If the thief had been a real criminal, or someone in need, he knew Lacy would have had a far different reaction. That at least would have been explainable and certainly far less disillusioning. He followed her out of the car and into her apartment.

"He's not worth it," he said vehemently, taking her shoulders so that she had to look at him. "Don't let him hurt you this way."

"I'm not hurt," Lacy denied instinctively, though in her heart she knew he spoke the truth.

"Aren't you?" David glared at her. "I never doubted your honesty until now."

Stung, Lacy tried to draw back. "Just what does that mean?" Temper came out of nowhere to catch her unaware. Frustration uncoiled within her, snapping, clouding the need with emotions of the past, feelings no one knew she had, feelings she had buried in self-defense. Color surged under her skin. Her eyes spit fire as she stared at the man who dared to tell her she hurt.

"You know what it means." Damn. Couldn't she see she was tearing herself up over something that she couldn't change? What fool had ever encouraged her in this insanity she called a job? She was too soft, too idealistic for this work. She had courage and drive, but not the heart for it.

Lacy jerked out of his hold. "I'm too tired to talk in riddles." She turned to the window, giving him her back. She wasn't strong enough to force him to leave, but she could make her point in other ways.

David was past control, past giving her time to understand herself, to see the things he saw about her career and the life she was forcing on herself. "Then I'll make it clearer. Quit this damn insanity and marry me. Let me take you away from drug addicts, bums, meetings in the dark of night with nothing for protection but a gun. You won't ever have to see ugliness or cruelty again. There won't be any more stupid midnight stakeouts, either. You'll sleep when you want, go when you want and have more than you've ever dreamed of." Long before he was done, the anger had died in his voice and was replaced by love and an impassioned plea for her to care more for him than for the job that had always come first in her life.

Lacy heard only words, words spoken in different forms, by different people all through her life. She saw a candy cane held out to one who knew that bright-colored sugar treats never fed a body or a mind. The values, the sensitivity, the emotion that she had thought David possessed disappeared as though they had never been. Anger and past pain obscured the truth, opening the way for damning words. She swung around, her eyes bright with emotion unchecked.

"If you believe I want to be a kept woman for the rest of my days, married or not, then we don't know each other at all. You're no better than Charles, and you would make me no better as well."

She could not have insulted him more. David inhaled sharply, feeling the pain of her renunciation slice through to his soul.

"Take that back," he snapped, his hands clenching at his sides.

Lacy lifted her head, stiffening at the command. "I never take back the truth."

"You wouldn't know the truth if it reached up and bit you on the nose," he shouted, trying to reach her. "You've lived in this dirty little world so long you don't know when someone really cares about you." He laughed grimly, too hurt to be kind. "You don't trust me or yourself. And you accuse me of buying you. Believe me, if I were going to buy a woman I could do better than a crazy female detective who didn't even know how to smile when I met her. You live in this damn house and there isn't anything personal here. No pictures, no clutter, no plants. Nothing that needs care. You can't cook, you have someone who cleans for you because you're never home. What kind of life is that for anyone, man or woman? Are you intending to grow old in this damn job, alone, unloved, unloving?" With each sentence he took a step closer, until the last brought him within inches of her rigid form.

Lacy was past anger. Rage swirled in dark waves. A need to slash back rose. She raised her hand to slap his face, anything to make him shut up. She couldn't, no, wouldn't take anymore. David caught her arm before she could connect. He held her eyes as he forced her arm down between them without letting it go.

"It only needed this to make the evening complete." David held her wrist. "If you want proof of what you are, it's here. You have the training to fight more effectively than this, but you didn't use it." He had control again. Her lashing out had given him that, at least. "Even in a rage you couldn't really hurt me. Can't you see that?"

Lacy stared at him, appalled at what she almost did. What she wanted to do. She had never struck out at someone in anger. "David, I..." she began, then stopped. She didn't know what to say. She stared at him, confused, more uncertain than she had ever been in her life. "What do you want from me?"

"I want you to see what you're doing to yourself." He touched her cheek. "Open your eyes, Lacy, for your own sake."

"You want me to give it up, don't you?" She didn't need his nod as she plunged on. "Well, I can't. And don't kid yourself it's for my sake. You don't like the danger. You told me that, or had you forgotten? You just don't understand."

David stared at her, realizing he had lost. All the time, the care he had taken hadn't worked. She couldn't or wouldn't see the truth. Defeat dragged at him. He released her because he had no choice. There was nothing here for him. His love had not been enough.

"I love you, but I won't watch you destroy yourself." He waited for a moment, hoping she would change her mind. When she only looked at him without a sign of softening he accepted he had failed. Without another word he turned away. A second later the door closed with a small click behind him.

Lacy stared at the door. Tears trickled down her face, but she didn't feel them. All she knew was the cold emptiness of being alone. Wrapping her arms around herself she sank to the floor on legs that would no longer support her weight. A sob tore from her throat, shocking her.

"I never cry," she whimpered, dashing the tears from her face. But still they fell, silent evidence of her grief. She had lost him. He would not be back. The laughter, the tenderness and the love was gone with him. She bowed her head, drowning in the solitude, the sorrow. The sun might rise tomorrow, but the day would be gray. The laughter was wrapped around the man who had loved her and walked away leaving her with the choice she had made.

Eleven

———

You look like the devil," John said bluntly as Lacy entered his office.

Lacy bit back an oath and sighed deeply. She had hoped her tears and the sleepless night would remain her secret. "You would, too, if you had spent half the night in the bushes and the other half trying to explain to the police department why you had set up a plan and not notified them of what you were doing," she excused herself, taking a chair. John didn't deserve her bad temper.

She slid a folder across the desk and then leaned back in her seat. Coming into the office this morning had taken more strength than she had thought she possessed. All she had wanted to do was to hide, try to pull herself together before she had to face the world again.

John stared at the thick report, surprised that she had it finished so quickly. "Correct me if I'm wrong, but isn't it just ten o'clock?"

"You know it is." Lacy made herself pay attention to the conversation.

"Then how?" He waved his hand at the folder.

"I couldn't sleep." A massive understatement if ever there was one. "I wanted to get the windup report out of the way as soon as possible, and since it was so late when I got in I decided to do it instead of sleeping."

John frowned. "It shows. We've got a meeting with Garrick this afternoon to bring him up-to-date. Maybe you'd better go home and get some rest first."

Lacy was shaking her head before he finished speaking. "You have the meeting. I would just as soon forego the pleasure of Ross Garrick if you don't mind."

Eyes intent on her face, John asked, "Meaning?"

Lacy shrugged, too tired to care that he wanted more of an explanation of her uncharacteristic behavior. She had never refused to be in on the final interview with a client before, and they both knew it. "John, I need some time off." She paused, then continued with more determination. An impulse had prompted the words, but now that Lacy had said them she knew she had spoken the truth. "Starting today."

John studied her, saying nothing for a long minute. In all the years Lacy had been with him he couldn't remember her looking, acting or sounding the way she did now. There was an air of defeat or discouragement surrounding her. "Why? What happened last night? Is it the case, or did something happen between you and Marsh? If he hurt you…" He braced his hands on the desk and started to get to his feet.

Her life was falling about her in great chunks. Nothing was as it should be. She hurt deep down to her soul. "Sit down, John," Lacy commanded tiredly. "It's not David. It's me. I'm burned out. I need some time off, and this thing with Garrick and Osgood just made me see that, that's all." The small lie hardly mattered, Lacy assured herself silently as she awaited John's verdict. The season was still with them as were the demands it made on the agency. To take time now was to leave John shorthanded. She hated asking for a break, but she knew she had to have one.

John slowly relaxed, knowing Lacy well enough to realize she wouldn't have made the request unless the need was great. "Talk to me," he murmured finally.

"There isn't anything more to say. Not really." The only man she wanted to talk to was David and he was gone. She felt the sting of tears yet again and damned the rawness of her emotions. She couldn't break down here.

John studied her for a long moment before inclining his head. "Lacy, you know I'm here." Something was terribly wrong. His niece was not a woman who gave into tears, but for a second they had been in her eyes. Suddenly he saw the heavy makeup he hadn't noticed earlier. Camouflage. The relaxed position she held wasn't relaxed at all. It, too, was a pretense.

Lacy knew he was looking for answers beyond the words she spoke. They were too close, too alike, for her not to know. She could lie even more than she had done, but didn't. "I stood there last night, John, and listened to Osgood explain in a perfectly reasonable way why he had done what he did. Not for money or revenge or need, but for amusement. It made me sick just to hear him. He really thinks he can do what he did and get away with it.

Do you know he even planned how to return what he had taken? He is not the least bit remorseful. But worst of all, with enough money and a top-notch lawyer, he might get off with a slap on the wrist. His reputation will suffer for a while, but even that will probably blow over." This much of the truth she could give him. This much of her feelings he could understand.

"Probably," John agreed, not hearing the evasion for what it was. "But you know this work isn't exactly meant to restore anyone's faith in humanity. We only see the worst of people as a rule. What's so different now?"

"I don't know." Lacy spread her hands trying to explain what she didn't fully understand herself. She was terrified to admit that she had begun to see what David had tried to tell her. "That's why I need time away from here. I need to think. Really think. Decide if I want out."

John's head lifted with a snap, shock evident on his face. "Out? As in find another line of work?"

"Yes."

One simple word and it could mean the end of a career that she had been sure she always wanted and had been good at. Lacy hadn't realized until she said it that she was even thinking along those lines. It wasn't a break she needed so much as it was a direction. David had made her think, feel and touch something beyond the work she did. He had changed her in ways she had not noticed or expected.

"All right. If this is what you need, then you should go." He paused, then continued. He was really worried now, but tried not to show it. Lacy had enough to contend with. "How long?"

"I don't really know." Lacy couldn't make herself care.

"Why don't you take three weeks. You haven't had a vacation in years." If it took rearranging the whole office he would give her what she needed. He loved her, and if she hurt he wanted to help even if he couldn't see the problem as she did.

"Are you sure? That would put us at the end of the tourist season."

"It doesn't matter. You're more important to me."

It took every ounce of willpower Lacy possessed not to cry. John had always been there for her. He hadn't always known exactly what to do with the teenager he had taken to raise, but he had tried. "Maybe I could wait until after Easter when all the snowbirds fly back home," she offered, guilt pushing the suggestion out.

John's temper flared then. "No way. You do what you must. We'll be all right. In fact, you have just given me a perfect excuse to work on a case that has me intrigued."

"It was going to be mine, wasn't it?" Lacy deduced immediately. She had to talk to keep her mind off her seesawing emotions until escape was possible. She rose as John did and headed for the door.

"It was, but now it's mine."

"You quit fieldwork five years ago."

"By choice and you know it. Don't try to make this into some noble sacrifice." He gave her a glare that fooled neither of them.

Lacy felt a welling of love for this man who had raised her. On impulse she hugged him close. John's face was a picture of shock. He patted her shoulder awkwardly. Neither of them had ever been very demonstrative, and he wasn't sure how to handle her spontaneous show of affection.

"Go home," he ordered gruffly.

Lacy retreated a step, smiling slightly at his anxious look. "I'm all right," she said, trying to ease his mind.

Lacy left the agency and headed home. She showered and changed into her oldest clothes without thought. Feeling empty, she went to the kitchen for something to eat. Scrambled eggs and bacon was one of the few things she could do in the kitchen with marginal success. Lacy got out a skillet and opened the refrigerator. She sighed deeply when almost-bare shelves stared back at her. One egg carton sat crosswise on the upper level, but there was no bacon. Grabbing the carton without checking the contents she opened the freezer. There was a little more there than in the fridge but still no bacon.

Irritated, Lacy swore once before slamming the door. A tear splashed on her hand, and she wiped it away with an angry swipe. "I'll just have three eggs instead of two," she muttered, collecting the butter and reaching in the bread box for bread. "And I'll go grocery shopping this afternoon before I starve." Her hand encountered nothing but air and a few crumbs.

Empty! She couldn't take much more of this. First her job and now her home. Not home—house. She glanced around, seeing the room with a stranger's eyes. David was right. It was as impersonal as a damn hotel room. She sniffed inelegantly.

Slamming the carton of eggs on the counter, the lid popped off. For one second there was a pair of eggs inside. The force of her temper was stronger than the gravity that held the white duo in place. Both flipped out and hit the counter with a splat. Yellow and white yuck oozed over the counter. Lacy stared at the mess. It was the last straw. The tears couldn't be held back any longer.

"I need a keeper. Someone to hold my hand. I need David." The cry was pulled from the depths of her being. There in the kitchen, looking down at a splattered eggy glop she realized what had been staring her in the face all along.

She loved David. He had given her laughter, passion, tenderness, caring and, most of all, understanding. He had seen what she could not and had been strong enough to face her with the truth. He hadn't demanded of her even then. He had tried to reason, to help her know herself. And she had repaid him with anger, pain and rejection. The tears fell harder with every memory of the night before. She had shared her body and withheld her heart.

The doorbell rang but she didn't hear it. All she knew or heard was the sound of her own pain. It was only when she felt his hands on her arms lifting her to him, that she realized David had come back to her. He still cared.

"David!" she whispered, trying to stem the flow enough to really see his expression. She touched his face, his lips with her fingertips.

"What are you doing to yourself, little fool?" He groaned, pulling her into his arms where she should have been all along. "I leave you alone for a minute, and you tear yourself and this place up."

"It wasn't a minute. It was eight hours and fourteen minutes," she cried, slipping her arms around his neck. She would not let him go this time.

"Don't be precise. Not now." David took her lips, tasting the tears and the need. He had come prepared to fight for her. Now he only wanted to hold her forever. Time disappeared when he had her in his arms. Questions. Answers. For now it was enough she wanted him.

Lacy gave herself up to the passion and the joy he created for her. He was back. That was all that mattered. When he lifted his head, her tears had dried in silvery streaks.

"I didn't mean those things I said," she whispered, driven to taking back as much as she could of the anger, the pain and the rejection she had given him.

David stroked the tangled hair back from her temples. "I bungled things badly last night, honey, and hurt us both." He shook his head over his own stupidity. "I pushed you when I should have been listening to you. And I put what I felt in the worst possible light." He smiled sadly, watching her face, seeing her confusion. "I love you just the way you are. I don't want you to give up your life to join me in mine. I want us to share. I admit I don't think you're cut out for the work you do and that it scares me to think of the risks you take, but if that's what you need then it's what you must do."

"But don't you see?" Lacy caught his shoulders and shook him once. "You were right, and I was too locked into my rut to see it." She took a deep breath, trying to stem the words pouring out. "I hate so much of what I do. All the ugliness, the lies, the cruelties and the pettiness. I love the challenge of the work but not the realities of how I solve the puzzles. Until you came along, I was dying inside trying to be unemotional, detached and hard. I'm just not that. I want to smile, to see something good in this world we live in. But most of all I don't want to be alone anymore. You taught me how empty that is." She searched his face. Would it be enough?

David was stunned at the impassioned confession. Filled with pride, too, at the courage of the woman he loved. "What do you want to do?" It was her choice. It always had been.

"I don't know." She dropped her head on his chest. "I can't think. Detective work is all I have ever done."

David pulled her tight against him. "Don't sound so lost, love."

Lacy raised her head, almost bumping it on his chin. "Do you mean that?"

He frowned at her. "Mean what?"

"Love. Do you love me?"

He stared at her, unable to believe she had asked. Then he saw the uncertainty in her eyes, hope and traces of fear, too. He swept her into his arms. "So much that I am and was willing to swallow my pride." He took a step toward the door leading to the hall. "Apologize." Another two steps. "And beg if I had to, so that you would let me into your life with or without your damnable career." He mounted the stairs to her bedroom. "Ask me how many minutes there are in eight hours and fourteen minutes. Ask me how cold a night is without you. Ask me what laughter sounds like when I'm alone. And ask me what fear haunts me in the dead of night." He dropped her on the bed and came down beside her. "I was afraid, Lacy. More afraid than I have ever been in my life. I wasn't sure you would take me and my love and love me back." He unbuttoned her blouse and slipped it off her shoulders. "Do I love you? As long as I breathe and after. The question should be, do you love me?"

Tears filled her eyes, blurring his face. She brushed them away. Nothing, not even her tears, would hide him from her again. She didn't have it in her to be as eloquent as he. One day she would, but for now she only had an unvarnished truth. "I do."

He threw back his head, his laughter ringing out. Relief and deep love echoed in the sound. "Remember those words. Sometime in the very near future you'll need them both together."

She laughed with him, loving him, wanting him, needing him. Wrapping her arms around him she pulled him down. She sobered, staring into his eyes. His hands framed her face. "Tell me, love."

"I'm still scared. I can't promise I won't pine for the past or remember things I'd rather forget. I don't know what to do with my life."

"We'll find the answers. Remember I'm good at puzzles, too." The time for talk was done. The road ahead was far from clear, but it was bright with hope and promise. He had his woman. Now he would make her his love.

He bent his head, taking the lips she offered him. Lacy met him halfway. She needed this as much as she knew he did. What had gone before was a pale shadow across the moon compared to the desire that flared to life between them. The barriers were down.

Lacy came to him, joyously, freely. Beauty and happiness were in the smile he kissed from her lips. Pleasure was in the sound of her cries as he stroked her bare length, lingering over the intimate little places he knew as well as he knew his own heart. He was ready to love her but still he held back, wanting to prolong their moments together to savor to the last drop the sweetness of new love.

Lacy's hands trailed rivers of fire down his back and still he pleasured her and himself, smiling, loving her. "Slowly, love."

"I'm never slow," she whispered, too caught up in the storm he created to wait. She wanted to drink from him, of him until they were no longer two but one. "I love you. Don't make me wait." She pulled him to her, guiding him to complete their union.

David buried himself deep in her. He groaned as she closed her legs around him. Her fingers dug into his shoulders as Lacy arched beneath him, crying out at his possession.

"Closer," he whispered. "I can't get close enough to you." He moved against her again and again. "Say it, Lacy." The command was born out of his need to know she was real, that she did love him.

"I love you," Lacy breathed deeply.

One hand lifted to tangle in her hair. "I love you, woman." His lips covered hers with a passion that contained an element of savagery. His tongue entered, ravaged and possessed. *She* was possessed, a part of him both physically and emotionally.

Tension built in Lacy, drawing her breath from her body. So full. Fire. Sensation, an aching need for more. Whimpering, driving for the center of the storm that pulled at her, Lacy whispered words that promised, teased and commanded. Her man. Her lover. Her David. And then together they were there. The world splintered in a thousand pieces and a second later re-formed.

Lacy lay satiated in David's arms. She could not have moved so much as an eyelash if her life depended on it. David lifted himself from her arms, rolling onto his side and gathering her close. He wasn't ready to let her go, even now.

"Why didn't you give up on me?" she asked.

David tucked her hair behind her ear, lightly tracing the delicate whorls before answering. "I don't know. In the beginning I guess it was stubbornness. Then I got to know you and I was caught."

"I don't see how. We're miles apart." She managed to turn her head to look into his eyes. "I can't cook."

He smiled at that. "I've got a perfectly adequate cook and even if I didn't, I'd learn so we wouldn't starve."

"Greater love hath no man," she teased, smiling at him.

"Not exactly, love of my life. It's just after seeing that mess downstairs I value my digestive system too much...."

Lacy found energy she didn't know she had. She raised up on one elbow and tickled him. He yelped and grabbed at her hands. Laughing, she pushed him away. "I'll teach you to insult my cooking."

David caught her before she could slide out of bed. "Woman, you just started a war you can't hope to win." He pinned her to the mattress. "Besides, I was only stating the truth and you know it."

"In a pig's eye." Lacy gave her love a very un-loverlike look. "Just for that I've decided that while I'm trying to figure out what to do with my life *I* intend to take cooking lessons."

"Over my dead body."

She grinned at him with too much wickedness for him to doubt she intended to do what she said. "Wanna bet?" She raised her eyebrows.

He groaned, then smiled with a wickedness of his own.

Lacy saw the gleam in his eye just before he lowered his head to take her lips. She was breathing hard when he lifted his head again. "That won't stop me."

David didn't waste time with words.
Lacy got her cooking lessons, but he kept the cook.

*   *   *   *   *

Gary Hart, former Democratic senator for Colorado,
has written a frighteningly authentic tale
of man's race toward destruction.

GARY HART

In a world of international power politics, it becomes a race
against time as conspiracy and intrigue surround forces in Wash-
ington and Moscow that are attempting to sabotage the arms
negotiations.

"well-placed plot twists and sharp, believable dialogue"
—Booklist

"an intriguing plot"
—Philadelphia Inquirer

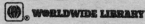

Silhouette Romance™
Legendary Lovers Trilogy

BY DEBBIE MACOMBER....

ONCE UPON A TIME, in a land not so far away, there lived a girl, Debbie Macomber, who grew up dreaming of castles, white knights and princes on fiery steeds. Her family was an ordinary one with a mother and father and one wicked brother, who sold copies of her diary to all the boys in her junior high class.

One day, when Debbie was only nineteen, a handsome electrician drove by in a shiny black convertible. Now Debbie knew a prince when she saw one, and before long they lived in a two-bedroom cottage surrounded by a white picket fence.

As often happens when a damsel fair meets her prince charming, children followed, and soon the two-bedroom cottage became a four-bedroom castle. The kingdom flourished and prospered, and between soccer games and car pools, ballet classes and clarinet lessons, Debbie thought about love and enchantment and the magic of romance.

One day Debbie said, "What this country needs is a good fairy tale." She remembered how well her diary had sold and she dreamed again of castles, white knights and princes on fiery steeds. And so the stories of Cinderella, Beauty and the Beast, and Snow White were reborn....

Look for Debbie Macomber's *Legendary Lovers* trilogy from Silhouette Romance: *Cindy and the Prince* (January, 1988); *Some Kind of Wonderful* (March, 1988); *Almost Paradise* (May, 1988). Don't miss them!

SRT-1

Silhouette Intimate Moments

NEXT MONTH
CHECK IN TO
DODD MEMORIAL HOSPITAL!

Not feeling sick, you say? That's all right, because Dodd Memorial isn't your average hospital. At Dodd Memorial you don't need to be a patient—or even a doctor yourself!—to examine the private lives of the doctors and nurses who spend as much time healing broken hearts as they do healing broken bones.

In UNDER SUSPICION (Intimate Moments #229) intern Allison Schuyler and Chief Resident Cruz Gallego strike sparks from the moment they meet, but they end up with a lot more than love on their minds when someone starts stealing drugs—and Allison becomes the main suspect.

In May look for AFTER MIDNIGHT (Intimate Moments #237) and finish the trilogy in July with HEARTBEATS (Intimate Moments #245).

Author Lucy Hamilton is a former medical librarian whose husband is a doctor. Let her check you in to Dodd Memorial—you won't want to check out!

IM229-1